Susan Stephens

THE SPANISH
BILLIONAIRE'S MISTRESS

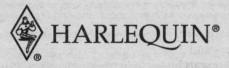

HARLEQUIN®

TORONTO • NEW YORK • LONDON
AMSTERDAM • PARIS • SYDNEY • HAMBURG
STOCKHOLM • ATHENS • TOKYO • MILAN • MADRID
PRAGUE • WARSAW • BUDAPEST • AUCKLAND

ISBN 0-373-12540-2

THE SPANISH BILLIONAIRE'S MISTRESS

First North American Publication 2006.

This edition published by arrangement with Harlequin Books S.A.

® and TM are trademarks of the publisher. Trademarks indicated with ® are registered in the United States Patent and Trademark Office, the Canadian Trade Marks Office and in other countries.

www.eHarlequin.com

Printed in U.S.A.

HARLEQUIN®
Presents

As the summer approaches we've got the reads to raise your temperature in Harlequin Presents!

Don't miss the first book in an exciting new trilogy, ROYAL BRIDES, by favorite author Lucy Monroe. *The Prince's Virgin Wife* is a tale of an irresistible alpha prince, an innocent virgin and the passion that ignites between them. In part two of Julia James's glamorous MODELS & MILLIONAIRES duet— *For Pleasure...or Marriage?*—enter a world of sophistication and celebrity, populated by beautiful women and a gorgeous Greek tycoon! *Captive in His Bed* is part two of Sandra Marton's Knight Brothers trilogy. This month we follow the passionate adventures of tough guy Matthew. And watch out, this story is in our UNCUT miniseries and that means it's *hot!*

We've got some gorgeous European men for you this month. *The Italian's Price* by Diana Hamilton sees an Italian businessman go after a woman who's stolen from his family, but what will happen when desire unexpectedly flares between them? In *The Spanish Billionaire's Mistress* by Susan Stephens, a darkly sexy Spaniard and a young Englishwoman clash. He thinks she's just out for her own gain—yet the physical attraction between them is too strong for him to stay away. In *The Wealthy Man's Waitress* by Maggie Cox, a billionaire businessman falls for a young Englishwoman and whisks her off to Paris for the weekend. He soon discovers that she is not just a woman for a weekend....

Check out www.eHarlequin.com for a list of recent Presents books! Enjoy!

Dear Reader,

A couple of years ago I was staying at a family-run hotel in a remote, mountainous region of Spain. I was walking back up the hill one evening when an ancient camper van chugged past me. Out of this van climbed a stout, middle-aged Spanish woman, a wiry old man carrying a battered guitar case and two slim, shy young girls.

When we sat down to eat at tables set out on the stone patio, it was beautifully warm. The only light came from the moon and from the many candles. A chord, beautifully played on the guitar, drew everyone's attention. A stately figure dressed all in black stepped in front of us. It was the woman from the van—only she had been transformed into a most marvelous, electrifying figure. The two shy young girls joined her on the improvised stage, but they too held themselves differently now, with great style and élan.

That evening will stay in my memory forever: the sensational flamenco dancing, the cries from the hearts of the participants, the soulful music played on an old guitar. You only had to see that guitar coming to life beneath the fingers of the elderly man to dream about all those other evenings just like this one, stretching up from his youth.

I was fortunate indeed to be there, to witness such talent and to share for just an evening such a heritage. I couldn't resist setting a romance in the mountains of Spain, far away from all the hustle and bustle of the coast. I hope you enjoy reading about the flamenco dancers and Zoë's encounter with them as much as I loved researching and writing this book.

Happy reading everyone!
Susan
www.susanstephens.net

All about the author...
Susan Stephens

SUSAN STEPHENS was a professional singer before
meeting her husband on the tiny Mediterranean
island of Malta. In true Presents style they met
on Monday, became engaged on Friday and were
married three months later. Almost thirty years and
three children later they are still in love. (Susan does
not advise her children to return home one day with
a similar story, as she may not take the news with
the same fortitude as her own mother!)

Susan had written several non-fiction books when
fate took a hand. At a charity costume ball there
was an after-dinner auction. One of the lots,
"Spend a Day with an Author," had been donated
by Harlequin Presents® author Penny Jordan.
Susan's husband bought this lot and Penny was to
become not just a great friend, but a wonderful
mentor who encouraged Susan to write romance.

Susan loves her family, her pets, her friends and her
writing. She enjoys entertaining, travel and going to
the theater. She reads, cooks and plays the piano to
relax, and can occasionally be found throwing
herself off mountains on a pair of skis or galloping
through the countryside.

Visit Susan's Web site at www.susanstephens.net—
she loves to hear from her readers all around
the world!

For all my long-suffering friends. You know who you are. I couldn't do it without you.

CHAPTER ONE

'COME here—come closer so we can see you,' the male voice commanded.

Cursing softly under her breath, Zoë Chapman slithered down to the ground and straightened up. Uncomfortable but invisible, or so she'd thought, she had been wedged into a smooth crevice between two giant rocks, discreetly observing the activity around the campfire.

She had located the flamenco camp and chosen her hiding place before anyone arrived. Her unique and popular cookery shows depended upon the co-operation of special interest groups, but the fact that she worked on a TV programme didn't make her welcome everywhere. She had wanted to observe the dancing before she introduced herself, just to make sure it was as good as was rumoured in the village.

The man speaking now had arrived shortly after she had. Back turned, he had stood gazing out across the valley. She had seen nothing more than an aggressively tall male figure, a shock of inky black hair and a wide sweep of shoulders—in fact, everything she had vowed to avoid since gaining her freedom.

As more people had joined him, she'd realised he was the leader of the group. Why hadn't she been surprised? She had wondered who he was, wondered about the quivers running through her as she stared at him. It had made her angry to think she had learned nothing since her divorce. She was still drawn to dangerous men.

Now, walking up to him, she saw he was everything she had expected: strikingly handsome, arrogant, and angry that she was here uninvited. If this hadn't been work she would have done the sensible thing, and left.

During the course of her television series she searched out interesting people from all walks of life. Local people in whichever country she chose to film were the seasoning in her shows, the magic ingredient that lifted her above the competition.

Generally she enjoyed the research. This time she had to put her personal feelings to one side and hope the dancing started soon. She couldn't let some local brigand put her off. Forget the man! This was her target group. The only thing that mattered was persuading someone to perform flamenco on her programme.

Dance was Zoë's passion outside of work. She knew she would never make a professional, but part of her climb-back after the divorce had been to join a jazz dance exercise group. It had proved the best therapy she could have chosen—though right now it looked as if all her good work was being undone.

She could not have prepared for this, Zoë reminded herself. She had not expected to run up against such a strong character again quite so soon.

'Well, what are you waiting for?'

He beckoned her forward with a short, angry gesture, and his voice was cold. It brought back memories she didn't need, but she was like a terrier with a bone when it came to work, and she focused her concentration easily. They were attracting a lot of attention. Perhaps one of the people around the mountain hut would agree to audition for her programme?

The man held up his hand to stop her coming any closer. It was close enough for Zoë, too. He was quite something. Along with the aura of power and brute strength, she had to admit he had style. Why did she have to find such a man irresistible when she knew he had danger carved into the stone where his heart should be?

Somewhere between thirty and thirty-five, he was around

six feet two or three, and his build was every bit as impressive as she had thought from some distance away. Everything about him was dark: his eyes, his hair…his expression.

'Why have you come here?' he demanded.

'I heard this is where flamenco enthusiasts gather, and I want to learn more about flamenco.'

'So you can go home to England and show off to your friends?' He made a derisive sound and clicked his fingers, mimicking the worst of the shows she had seen down on the coast.

'No, of course not. I…' His steely gaze remained fixed on her face, but she couldn't let that get to her. 'I am genuinely interested in flamenco.'

'Are you alone?'

'I am at the moment—'

He cut her off. 'At the moment?'

'I know this looks bad—'

'What do you mean, you're alone at the moment?'

'I'm working with a television crew. They're not here right now.'

Could his expression darken any more? She tried to explain, but her voice came out as a croak. Unconsciously, her hand flew to her throat. She should have brought some water with her. She had been at the mercy of the sun all afternoon, and now she was desperate for a drink.

'Do you think I could have some water?' She gazed around.

'What do you think this is? A café?'

But people were drinking all around her. 'I'm sorry, I—'

'Did you think this was one of those cheap tourist places where you get a free drink along with your *paella* and chips?'

'No!' She calmed herself. 'No, of course not—'

He straightened up and moved a menacing pace towards her, and all her courage drained away. Lurching backwards, she nearly stumbled. She was only saved by the sheer bulk of a man behind her. He was carrying a stone flagon and some pottery beakers. He didn't understand when she started to apologise, and poured her a drink.

She didn't want it. She just wanted to get away—back down the mountain to safety, to where people barely looked at her, where no one knew who she was or where she had come from.

But the man with the flagon was still smiling at her, and the situation was bad enough already. *'Gracias, señor.'*

Keeping watch on the brigand, Zoë took the beaker from the older man and gratefully drank from it.

It was delicious, and tasted harmless—like fruit juice and honey laced with some spice she couldn't name. The beaker felt cool, and she was so thirsty she didn't protest when he offered her more. The golden liquid gleamed in the light as it flowed from the flagon, and the elderly man filled her beaker to the brim.

'Salud!'

The alpha male's voice was harsh and unfriendly. Handing the beaker back to the man with the flagon, Zoë raised her chin. She felt better now, bolder. 'Delicious,' she said defiantly, staring her unwilling host in the eyes. 'What was that drink?'

'A local speciality, brewed here in the village.'

'It's very good. You should market it.'

'On your recommendation I'll certainly consider it.'

His sarcasm needled Zoë, but it also renewed her determination to go nowhere until she got the feature for her programme. At any cost?

At the cost of a little charm, at least. 'I really should introduce myself.'

'You really should.'

Brushing a strand of titian hair from her face, Zoë stared up and tried to focus. She hadn't realised the drink was so strong. On an empty stomach, she was suddenly discovering, it was lethal. She was in no state to object when he reached forward to steady her.

His grip on her arm was light, but even through an alcohol-induced haze she could feel the shock waves radiating out from his fingertips until every part of her was throbbing. He led her away out of earshot, to where a wooden hut cast some shade.

'So, who are you?'

'Zoë—Zoë Chapman. Could I have a glass of water, please?'

Rico thought he recognised the name, then brushed it aside. It hardly mattered. She had damned herself already out of her own mouth: a television crew! He might have known. He grimaced, catching hold of her again when she stumbled.

'I think you'd better sit down.' He steered her towards a bench, and once she was safely planted turned and called to two youths. 'José! Fernando! *Por favor, café solo—rápido!*' Then, turning to her again, he said, 'Welcome to the Confradias Cazulas flamenco camp, Zoë Chapman. Now you're here, what do you want?'

'It's good to meet you too—'

'Don't give me all this nonsense about flamenco. What do you really want? Why have you come here? Are you spying on me?'

'Flamenco isn't nonsense.' She reeled back to stare at him. 'And I'm not spying on you. I'm researching.'

'Oh, of course. I see,' he said sarcastically.

No, he didn't, Zoë thought, shading her eyes with her hand as she tried to focus on his face. Her head felt so heavy. It bounced instead of simply moving. Squeezing her eyes together, she struggled to follow his movements—he seemed to be swaying back and forth. 'So, who are you, then?' Her tongue was tied up in knots.

'Rico. Rico Cortes.'

They were attracting attention, Zoë noticed again. Peering

round him, she gave a smile and a little wave. He moved in
closer, shielding her from his companions. 'I'm very pleased
to meet you, Rico.' As she put her hand out to shake his, it
somehow connected with a coffee cup. Raising the cup to her
lips, she drank the coffee down fast. The hot, bitter liquid
scalded her throat, but it couldn't be helped. She had to pull
round from this fast. The last couple of programmes based
around flamenco were supposed to be the crowning feature of
her series.

'Here, drink some more.'

His voice was sharp, and then he made a signal to the boy
with the coffee pot to fill her mug again.

'Leave it here, José, *por favor.*'

He sounded different, warmer when he spoke to the youth,
Zoë registered fuzzily.

'We're going to need every drop,' he added.

And he was back to contempt when he turned to look at
her! It wasn't the best start she'd ever had to a programme.

This time, once she'd drained the strong black coffee, it
was Zoë who asked for more. The second she had finished,
the questions started.

'If you're with a television crew I take it you're after an
exclusive. I'm right, aren't I? That's why you were spying on
us, sneaking about.'

Thanking the boy, Zoë gave him back her empty cup. Her
head was clearing. She felt better, much more focused. She
might still be a little under par, but she had no intention of
being bullied by Rico Cortes—by anyone.

'I'm here to see if flamenco will make a suitable item for
my television series. Nothing more.'

'*Your* television series?'

'It's my programme. I have full editorial control. I own the
company that produces the programme.'

'So, it's you.'

'Me?'

'Staying at the Castillo Cazulas.'

'Yes, my company has taken a short-term lease on the castle—'

'And it's there you're going to create your masterpiece?'

'I beg your pardon?' She couldn't keep the chill out of her voice now. Could he have been more disparaging? She had worked long and hard to raise her programme above the rest, to make it different and special. She had brought a great team together, and she was proud of what they had achieved.

'Flamenco for Spain, opera in Italy, fashion when you shoot a programme in France—is that how it goes? Skimming over the surface of a country, using the name of art just to make money?'

'I make money. I won't deny it. How would I stay in business, pay the wages of the people who work with me, otherwise? But as for your other assumptions—frankly, they stink.'

'They do?'

His voice was faintly amused now, and he was looking at her in a whole different way. She wasn't sure if she liked it any better. Her thundering heart told her it was dangerous. 'Look, Rico, if you're not the person I should be speaking to about the dancing, then perhaps you could find me someone who will listen to what I have to say.'

'And allow you to trample over my privacy? I don't think so.'

'*Your* privacy? I wasn't aware that my programme was going to be made around you.'

His look was cynical. 'It's time you went back to your film crew, Ms Chapman.'

'Are you asking me to leave?'

'It's getting dark—I'd hate for you to lose your way.'

'Don't worry, I'll go. Just as soon as I finish my business here.'

'You *have* finished your business here.'

'Why are you so touchy about my being here? I'm not doing you any harm!'

'People have a right to space.'

'And this is yours?' Zoë gestured around.

'If you like. I don't have to explain myself to you.'

'Correct,' Zoë said, standing up to face him. 'But I wasn't aware that there were any private estates up here in the mountains. I've got as much right to be here as you have. And, for your information, I have never had a single complaint from a guest on my show. I treat everyone with respect.'

He shifted position and smiled. It was not a friendly smile. It was a 'don't mess with me' smile.

'I give you my word,' Zoë insisted. 'Nothing in my programme will invade your privacy—'

His short bark of laughter ran right through her, and his derision made her cheeks flame red.

'You really believe that?'

'Yes, of course I do.'

'Then you're dreaming.'

'Perhaps if you'd allow me to explain how everything works—'

'You still couldn't come up with anything to reassure me.'

This was her most challenging project yet. But she had never failed before. Not once. No one had ever refused to take part in one of her programmes, and she wasn't going to let Rico Cortes start a trend.

'Have the effects of that drink worn off yet?'

He couldn't wait to get rid of her, Zoë guessed. 'Yes, they have.' Hard luck. She was firing on all cylinders now.

He turned away. Evidently as far as Rico was concerned their discussion had come to an end. He couldn't have cared less about her programme—he just didn't want her blood on his hands when she tumbled over a cliff after drinking the local hooch at his precious flamenco camp. 'We haven't finished talking yet!' she shouted after him.

'I have.'

As he turned to stare at her Zoë wondered if he could sense the heat building up in her. His slow smile answered that question, and she wasn't sure if she was relieved or not when he walked back towards her. 'Please, let me reassure you. I don't pose a threat to you or to anyone else here. I'm just trying to—'

'Find out more about flamenco?'

'That's right.'

As their eyes met and locked Zoë shivered inwardly. Rico was exactly the type of man she had vowed to avoid. 'It's getting late.' She looked hopefully at the sky. 'Perhaps you are right. This isn't the time—'

'Don't let me drive you away,' he sneered.

She was painfully aware of his physical strength, but then something distracted her. A broken chord was played with great skill on a guitar, so soft it was barely discernible above the laughter and chatter—but this was what she had come for. Silence fell, and everyone turned towards a small wooden stage. Lit by torchlight, it had been erected on the edge of the cliff, where it could catch the slightest breeze from the valley.

'Since you're here, I suppose you might as well stay for the performance.'

Rico's invitation held little grace, but she wasn't about to turn it down.

He cut a path through the crowd, and Zoë followed him towards the front of the stage. She could see the man with the guitar now, seated on a stool at one corner of the stage, his head bowed in concentration as he embraced the guitar like a lover. Then an older woman walked out of the audience and went to join him. Resting her hands on her knees to help her make the steep ascent up the wooden steps to the stage, she looked her age, but when she straightened up Zoë saw an incredible transformation take place.

Giving the audience an imperious stare, the woman

snatched up her long black skirt in one hand and, raising the other towards the sky, she stamped her foot once, hard.

A fierce energy filled the air as the woman began her performance. Zoë had no idea that Rico was watching her. She was aware of nothing outside the dance.

'Did you feel it?' he murmured, close to her face, as the woman finished and the crowd went wild.

'Did I feel what?' she said, moving closer so he could hear.

'*Duende.*'

As he murmured the word she looked at his mouth. '*Duende.*' Zoë tasted the word on her own lips. It sounded earthy and forbidden, like Rico Cortes. She sensed that both had something primal and very dangerous at their core.

'You wanted real flamenco,' he said, drawing Zoë back to the purpose of her visit. 'Well, *this* is real flamenco. This is wild, impassioned art at its most extreme. Are you ready for that, Zoë Chapman?'

She heard the doubt in his voice. Perhaps he saw her as a dried-up husk, incapable of feeling passion of any sort—and why not? He wouldn't be the first man to think that. 'I'm just really grateful to have this chance to see flamenco at its best.'

'You don't see flamenco. You feel it.'

'I know that now.' He thought of her as a tourist out for a cheap thrill, Zoë realised. But she was a long way from the tourist trail here. She was a long way from her old life too— the old Zoë Chapman would have backed off without a fight, but there was no chance of that now. She knew what she could achieve, with or without a man at her side. And she hadn't come to Spain to be insulted. She had come to make a programme, a good programme. She wasn't going to let Rico Cortes distract her from that goal. 'Can you explain this word *duende* to me?'

'You'll know it when you feel it.'

'What—like an itch?'

'Like an orgasm.'

Zoë's mouth fell open. Not many things shocked her. OK, so she'd been less than reverent in response to his cutting remarks, but it had been a serious question. She had been right about him. Rico Cortes was a man of extremes—a man who was looking at her now with a brooding expression on his face, no doubt wondering if his shock tactics had been sufficient to scare her off.

'An emotional orgasm, you mean?' She was pleased with her composure under fire.

'That's right.'

There was a spark of admiration in his eyes. It gave her a rush—maybe because there was passion in the air long after the woman's performance had ended. Vibrations from the flamenco seemed to have mixed with his maleness, taking her as close to *duende* as she would ever get. She held his gaze briefly, to prove that she could, and found it dark and disconcerting. Her body was trembling with awareness, as if an electric current had run through her.

'So, you have taken a summer lease on Castillo Cazulas,' he said, staring down at her as if he knew what she was feeling. 'And you want to make a programme about flamenco. Why here, of all places? Hardly anyone outside the village knows about the Confradias Cazulas flamenco camp.'

'People who know about flamenco do. And I enjoyed the walk.'

'But how will you find your way back again? It's almost dark.'

He was right, but she was prepared. 'I have this.' Digging in her pocket, Zoë pulled out her flashlight. Suddenly it didn't seem adequate. She should have remembered how fast daylight disappeared in Spain. It was as if the sun, having blazed so vigorously all day, had worn itself out, and dropped like a stone below the horizon in minutes.

They both turned as some more dancers took the stage. They were all talented, but none possessed the fire of the first woman. She had already found her guest artist, Zoë realised, but she would still need an introduction.

Glancing up, she knew that Rico was her best chance. But there were man waves coming off him in torrents, and he smelled so good—like pine trees and wood smoke. His sexual heat was curling round her senses like a blanket. *And lowering her guard!* She hadn't come to Spain to indulge in an adolescent fantasy over some arrogant stud. Her interest in flamenco was purely professional. Work was all she cared about; a new man figured nowhere in her plans.

By the time the stage had cleared again it was pitch-dark, with no moon. Quite a few people had come by car, parking in a clearing not too far away. Zoë watched with apprehension as their headlights glowed briefly before disappearing into the night.

'You really think that little light of yours is going to be enough?' Rico said, as if reading her mind.

Zoë glanced at him. 'It will have to be.' Shoving her hands in the pockets of her track suit, she tilted her chin towards the stage. 'Was that the last performance for tonight?'

'You want more?'

'How much would it cost to hire someone like that first performer—the older woman?'

She saw an immediate change in his manner.

'All the money on earth couldn't buy talent like that. *You* certainly couldn't afford it.'

Zoë bit back the angry retort that flew to her lips. This was no time for temperament: everyone was leaving—the woman too, if she didn't act fast. Their gazes locked; his eyes were gleaming in the darkness. This man frightened her, and she knew she should turn away. But she couldn't afford to lose the opportunity.

'I'm sorry—that was clumsy of me. But you can't blame me for being carried away by that woman's performance—'

'Maria.' His voice was sharp.

'Maria,' Zoë amended. She felt as if she was treading on eggshells, but his co-operation was crucial. She generally made a very convincing case for appearing on the show. Right now, she felt like a rank amateur. There was something about Rico Cortes that made her do and say the wrong thing every time. 'Maria's performance was incredible. Do you think she would dance for me?'

'Why on earth would she want to dance for *you*?'

'Not for me, for my show. Do you think Maria would agree to dance on my programme?'

'You'd have to ask her yourself.'

'I will. I just wanted to know what you thought about it first.' Zoë suspected nothing happened in Cazulas without Rico's say-so.

'It depends on what you can offer Maria in return.'

'I would pay her, of course—'

'I'm not talking about money.'

'What, then?'

A muscle worked in his jaw. 'You would have to win her respect.'

Did he have to look so sceptical? 'And what do you think would be the best way to do that?'

They were causing some comment, Zoë noticed, amongst the few people remaining, with this exchange, conducted tensely head to head. It couldn't be helped. She had to close the deal. She wasn't about to stop now she had him at least talking about the possibility of Maria appearing on the show.

'You'd have to bargain with her.'

An opening! Maybe not a door, but a window—she'd climb through it. 'What do you suggest I bargain with?' She smiled, hoping to appeal to his better nature.

'Are *you* good at anything?' Rico demanded.

Apart, that was, from joining the hordes who spied on him and the idiots who thought an important part of his heritage had the same value as the cheap tourist tat along the coast.

She had manoeuvred him into starting negotiations with her, though. She was sharper than most. He should have got rid of her right away, but his brain had slipped below his belt.

He shouldn't have stayed away from Cazulas for so long. He should have kept a tighter hold on who was allowed into the village. But he had trusted such things to a management company. He wouldn't be doing that again.

'I don't just make programmes,' she said, reclaiming his attention. 'I present them.'

'I apologise.' He exaggerated the politeness. 'Apart from your ability to make programmes and present them, what do you have to bargain with that might possibly interest Maria?'

'I cook.'

Removing her hands from her pockets, she planted them on her hips. She smiled—or rather her lips tugged up at an appealing angle while her eyes blazed defiance at him. Her manner amused him, and attracted him too. 'You cook?'

'Is there something wrong with that?'

'No, nothing at all—it's just unexpected.'

'Well, I don't know what you were expecting.'

Just as well. He had been running over a few things that would definitely make it to the top of his wish list, and cooking wasn't one of them. Outsiders were practically non-existent in the mountains. It was a rugged, difficult terrain, and yet Zoë Chapman, with her direct blue-green gaze and her wild mop of titian hair, had come alone and on foot, with a flashlight as her only companion, to find—what had she expected to find?

Rico's eyes narrowed with suspicion. In his experience, women made careful plans; they didn't just turn up on the off chance. 'We'll discuss this some other time. I'll have someone see you home.'

'When I've spoken to Maria.'

Her mouth was set in a stubborn line. He liked her lips. He liked her eyes too—when they weren't spitting fire at him.

She was about five-five, lightly built—but strong, judging from her handshake. The rest was a mystery beneath her shapeless grey track suit. Maybe it was better that way. There were very few surprises left in life.

But this was one mystery parcel he had no intention of unwrapping. The gutter press could use subtle tactics to succeed. Zoë Chapman might be working for anyone—how did he know? The television company, even the programme she was supposed to be making, could all be a front. Cazulas was special—the one place he could get some space, some recreation—and no one was going to spoil that for him.

'So, you'll introduce me to Maria?'

She was still here? Still baiting him? Rico's jaw firmed as he stared at Zoë. The sensible thing to do would be to cut her, blank her out, forget about her. But she intrigued him too much for that. 'It's not convenient right now—'

'Who says so?'

'Maria!' Rico turned with surprise. 'I didn't hear you coming.'

'That is obvious.' The older woman's eyes were bright and keen as she stared curiously at Zoë. 'But now I am here why don't you introduce us, Rico?'

'She won't be staying—'

'I will!'

Maria viewed them both with amusement.

'I didn't think you would be interested in what Ms Chapman had to say,' Rico said with a dismissive shrug.

'So now you are thinking for me, Rico?'

There was a moment when the two of them stared at each other, unblinking, and then Rico pulled back. 'Maria Cassavantes—allow me to present Zoë Chapman to you.'

'Zoë,' Maria repeated, imbuing Zoë's name with new colour. 'I have heard rumours about your television programmes and I would like to talk to you. Forget Rico for a moment. Perhaps we can come to some arrangement?'

It was everything Zoë had hoped for—but forget about Rico? That was asking a bit too much. She saw him tense and she couldn't resist a quick glance of triumph.

Rico was seething. What was Maria thinking of? They knew nothing about this Zoë Chapman—nothing at all. What set her apart from all the other female sharks, with their bleached teeth and avaricious natures? Maria hadn't a clue what she was letting herself in for—she was playing with fire…

'We should know more about your cookery programme before Maria agrees to do anything.' He took a step forward, deliberately putting himself between them. 'I don't see how flamenco could possibly be relevant.'

'If you'd only let me explain—'

'How can I be sure you're not wasting Maria's time?'

'I said I don't mind this, Rico.' Maria put a restraining hand on his arm. 'I would like to talk to Zoë and hear what she's got to say—'

'I promise you, Maria,' Zoë cut in, 'I'm not in the habit of wasting anyone's time, least of all my own. And if you need me to prove it to you—'

'I really do.' It was Rico's turn to butt in.

Maria was forgotten as they glared at each other. Then Zoë broke eye contact, allowing him a brief moment of satisfaction.

'I'll make everyone in the village a meal,' she declared, gesturing extravagantly around the clearing. 'How does that suit you, Rico?'

Now he was surprised. 'That's quite an offer.' There was just enough doubt in his voice to provoke her, to brighten her green eyes to emerald and make her cheeks flare red.

'I mean it.'

'Fine.' He lifted up his hands in mock surrender, then dipped his head, glad of the opportunity to conceal the laughter brewing behind his eyes. Somehow he didn't think Ms

Chapman would appreciate humour right now. But there were about one hundred and sixty souls in the village. She would never pull it off.

Ms Chapman. Who knew what was behind a name?

Rico's gaze flew to Zoë's hands. Clean, blunt fingernails, cut short, but no ring, no jewellery at all. He drew an easing breath. That was all he needed to know. It gave him the freedom to overlook his vow never to court trouble on his own doorstep again. 'I shall look forward to it, Ms Chapman.'

'Rico,' Maria scolded him, 'why don't you call our new friend Zoë, as we're going to be working together?'

'So we *are* going to be working together, Maria?'

She sounded so excited. Rico ground his jaw and watched with concern as the two women hugged each other. Zoë Chapman wouldn't win *him* round so easily.

'I have never appeared on television,' Maria exclaimed.

'I'm going to make it special for you, Maria.'

Zoë's promise grated on him. If she let Maria down—

'I think we'll make a good team.' Maria looked at him and raised her eyebrows, as if daring him to disagree.

For now it seemed he had no choice in the matter. Zoë Chapman had won this round, but he would be waiting if she stepped out of line. Maria might have been taken in, but he wasn't so easily convinced. The thought of an artist of Maria's calibre appearing on some trivial holiday programme with a few recipes thrown in made him sick to his stomach.

As far as he was concerned, *Ms* Chapman had identified her quarry and had stopped at nothing until she got her own way. She was no innocent abroad. She had all the grit and determination of the paparazzi. That wary look he had detected in her eyes when she looked at him didn't fool him for a minute. It was all an act. She was as guilty as hell. But Maria was right. He wouldn't presume to make decisions for Maria Cassavantes, though in his experience third-rate television companies only dealt in plastic people; treasures like Maria were out of their league.

If he had to, he would step in to protect her from Zoë Chapman. But for now he was sufficiently intrigued to give Ms Chapman enough rope to hang herself. He would watch her like a hawk, and the first time she tried to cheapen or trivialise what Maria Cassavantes stood for both she and her television cameras would be thrown out of Spain.

CHAPTER TWO

'CAN we talk business now, Maria?'

'That sounds very formal,' Rico cut in.

He was suspicious of her motives. She had to curb her enthusiasm, take it slowly, Zoë reminded herself. She usually got to know people first, before talking business. Building confidence was crucial. Contrary to popular opinion, not everyone wanted to appear on television. Usually she was good at choosing the right moment, but having Rico in the picture was making her edgy, making her rush things.

'I know it's late—I won't keep you long.' She glanced at Rico. 'Perhaps if Maria and I could talk alone?'

'It's all right, Rico,' Maria said soothingly.

'I'd rather stay.'

Zoë looked up at him. 'It's really not necessary.'

'Nevertheless.' He folded his arms.

For Maria's sake Zoë tried to bite back her impatience, but she was tired and stressed and the words just kept tumbling out. 'Really, Rico, I can't see any reason why you should stay. Maria and I are quite capable of sorting this out between us—'

'It's better if I stay.'

She could see he was adamant. 'Are you Maria's manager?'

'They call him El Paladín,' Maria cut in, interposing her not inconsiderable body between them.

'El Paladín?' Zoë repeated. 'Doesn't that mean The Champion?' She only had a very basic knowledge of conversational Spanish to call upon. 'What's that for, Rico? Winning every argument?'

'Rico is everyone's champion,' Maria said fondly, patting his arm.

That seemed highly unlikely—especially where she was concerned, Zoë thought. 'Champion of what?' she pressed.

'Zoë likes her questions,' Rico observed sardonically, 'but she's not too keen on giving answers about why she's really here in Cazulas—'

'And Zoë's right about you,' Maria cut in. 'You don't like losing arguments, Rico.'

'I like to win,' he agreed softly.

Lose? Win? Where was all this leading? Zoë wondered, suppressing a shiver as she broke eye contact with Rico. 'We're never going to win Rico's approval, Maria, but I believe we can make great television together.'

'What have you been telling this young woman, *malvado*?' Maria demanded, turning her powerful stare on him.

'Nothing. If you want to dance and she wants to cook, that's fine by me. Only problem is, we know *you* can dance.'

'Rico!' Maria frowned at him.

'My third television series says I can cook!'

'There—you see, Rico,' Maria said, smiling at Zoë.

'And the connection between dancing and cooking is what, exactly?' He raised his shoulders in a shrug as he stared at Zoë.

He would never go for her idea, but at least she had Maria's support. She had to forget Rico's insults and build on what she had. But he was one complication she could do without. He probably crooked his finger and every woman around came running. Well, not this woman.

Turning to Maria, Zoë deliberately cut him out. 'This is the connection, Maria: the people around me inspire the food I cook on television. In this part of Spain the influence of flamenco is everywhere.'

'So cooking isn't just a hobby for you?' Rico said.

Zoë stared up at him. He refused to be cut out. 'No, Rico, it's a full-time career for me.'

'Along with your television company.'

Maria stepped between them again. 'So you would like me to dance on your television programme to add some local interest to the dishes you prepare? Is that right, Zoë?'

'Exactly.' Zoë's face was confident as she flashed a glance at Rico. 'I'll cook, you'll dance, and together we'll make a great team.'

'*Bueno,*' Maria said approvingly. 'I like the sound of this programme of yours. Of course, any payment must be donated to the village funds.'

'Absolutely,' Zoë agreed. 'Whatever you like.'

Maria smiled. 'Well, that all sounds quite satisfactory to me.'

But not to Rico, Zoë thought. At least he was silent for now. 'I have never seen anyone dance like you, Maria. You are fantastic.'

'*Gracias*, Zoë. And you are very kind.'

'Not kind, Maria, just honest.' Zoë stopped, hearing Rico's scornful snort in the background. What did she have to do to convince him?

She turned to look at him coldly. There were a couple of buttons undone at the neck of his dark linen shirt, showing just how tanned and firm he was. She turned back quickly to Maria. 'When you appear, I just know the programme will come to life…' Zoë's voice faded. She could feel Rico's sexual interest lapping over her in waves.

'Don't worry, Zoë,' Maria assured her, filling the awkward silence. 'It will be fine—just you wait and see.'

Zoë wasn't so sure, and she was glad of Maria's arm linked through her own as the older woman drew her away from Rico, towards the bright circle of light around the campfire.

'Have you offered Zoë a drink?' Maria said, turning back to him.

'She's had more than enough to drink already.'

'Surely you didn't let her drink the village liquor?'

'It's all right, Maria,' Zoë said hastily. She could see the hard-won progress she had made winning Maria's trust vanishing in the heat of a very Latin exchange. 'Thank you for the kind offer, but I've already had some coffee.'

Rico was staring at her almost as if he was trying to remember why she made him so uneasy. But they couldn't have met before. And he couldn't know about her past; she was anonymous in the mountains. Television reception was practically non-existent, and there were no tabloid papers on sale at the kiosk in the village.

'So, Zoë, when do I dance for you?' Maria said, reclaiming Zoë's attention.

'How about Tuesday?' Zoë said, turning back to thoughts of work with relief. 'That gives us both time to prepare.'

'Tuesday is good for me.' Maria smiled broadly as she broke away. 'On Tuesday you cook, and I dance.'

'Are you sure you know what you're taking on, Zoë?'

Rico's words put a damper on their enthusiasm.

'Why? Don't you think I'm up to it?'

'It's *what* you're up to that I'm more interested in.'

'Then you're going to have a very dull time of it,' Zoë assured him. 'I'm going to cook and Maria is going to dance. I don't know what you're imagining, but it really is as simple as that.'

'In my experience, nothing is ever that simple.'

Zoë's gaze strayed to his lips: firm, sensuous lips that never grew tired of mocking her.

'Today is Saturday—no, Sunday already,' Maria said with surprise, staring at her wristwatch. 'It is well past midnight. I have kept you far too long, Zoë.'

'That's not important,' Zoë assured Maria, turning to her with relief. 'All that matters is that you're happy—you're the most important person now. I want to make sure you have everything you need on the night of your performance.'

'Such as?' Maria said.

'Well—would you like to eat before or after you dance?'

'Both. I need to build up my strength.' She winked at Zoë. 'Some people don't need to build up strength, of course.' She shot a glance at Rico. 'But you had better feed him anyway. I'm sure he'd like that.'

'I'm sure he would.' Zoë's gaze veered coolly in Rico's direction. She might find him a few sour grapes.

'Don't take me for granted, Zoë,' he said, 'I might not even be there.'

'Don't worry, Rico. Where you're concerned I won't take anything for granted. I'll expect you at the castle around nine?' she confirmed warmly with Maria.

'And I will dance for your cameras at midnight.'

Zoë felt a rush of pleasure not even Rico could spoil. She had accomplished her mission successfully, and there was a bonus—she had made a new friend in Maria. She just knew Maria would have what they called 'screen magic', and the programme in which she featured would be unique.

'Rico, would you make sure that everyone in the village knows they are welcome to come and eat at Castillo Cazulas and celebrate Maria's performance on Tuesday night?' Zoë said, turning to him.

For a moment he was amazed she had included him in her arrangements. He had to admit he admired her guts—even if she did annoy the hell out of him. He should be there, just to keep an eye on her.

In fact, he could take a look around right now if he drove her back to the castle. Time to turn on the charm.

'Don't worry, no one loves a party more than we do in Cazulas—isn't that right, Maria?' He looked at Zoë. 'You'll be calling in extra help, I imagine?'

There was something in Rico's eyes Zoë didn't like.

Something that unnerved her. 'There's no need. I'm not alone at the castle, Rico. I have my team with me—and don't forget that cooking is what I do for a living.'

Turning away from him, she said her goodbyes to Maria, all the time conscious of Rico's gaze boring into her back. He might as well have gripped her arms, yanked her round, and demanded she give him her life history. She could only think that having a woman set both the rules and the timetable was something entirely new to him.

'How are you going to get home tonight, Zoë?' Maria said.

'I'll drive her back.'

'I'll walk.'

Maria frowned, looking from Rico to Zoë and back again. 'Of course you will drive Zoë home, Rico.' She put her arm around Zoë's shoulder. 'It is too dangerous for you to walk, Zoë, and you will be quite safe with Rico—I promise you.'

There was something in Maria's eyes that made Zoë want to believe her. But as she walked away Zoë could have kicked herself. Why hadn't she just asked if she could take a lift with Maria?

'Are you ready to go?' Rico said.

'I thought we'd already been through this.' Digging in her pocket, Zoë pulled out her flashlight again.

'Oh, that's right. I had forgotten you were an intrepid explorer.'

'I'll only be retracing my steps—'

'In the dark.'

'Well, I'd better get going, then.'

She moved away, and for one crazy moment hoped he would come after her. When he did she changed her mind. 'I'll be fine, Rico. Really.'

'What are you afraid of, Zoë? Is there something at the castle you don't want me to see?'

'Is that what you think?' She ran her hand through her hair

as she looked at him. 'I can assure you I have nothing to hide. Come around and check up on me if you don't believe me.'

'How about now?'

'I'd rather walk.'

'Well, I'm sorry, Maria's right. I can't let you do that. It's far too dangerous.'

Maria hadn't left yet. Her friend's truck was still parked in the clearing. She might just catch them. But Maria moved as fast as she had on the stage. Climbing into the cab, she slammed the door and waved, leaving Zoë standing there as the truck swung onto the dirt road leading down to the village and accelerated away.

'Don't look so worried.'

Don't look so worried? I'm stuck at the top of a mountain in the middle of the night with a flashlight and the local brigand—who happens to have a chip on his shoulder labelled 'media-types/female'—and I shouldn't worry?

'Like I said, I'll drive you back.'

'No way!'

'You can cut the bravado, Zoë—there's no moon, hardly any path, and this stupid little light won't save you when you're plunging down a precipice.'

'Give that back to me now.' Zoë made a swipe for her flashlight, but Rico was too quick for her.

'It's no trouble for me to drop you at the castle.'

'Thank you, I'll walk.'

She got as far as the rock-strewn trail leading down to the valley before he caught hold of her arm and swung her around.

'You are not going down there on your own.'

'Oh, really?'

'Yes, really.'

Their faces were too close. As their breath mingled Zoë closed her eyes. 'Let go of me, Rico.'

'So you can mess up a rock? So you can cause me a whole

lot of trouble in the morning when I have to come looking for your mangled body? I don't think so, lady.'

'Your concern is overwhelming, but I really don't need it! I know these mountains—'

'Like the back of your hand? And you've been here how long?'

'Nearly a month, as a matter of fact.' That silenced him, Zoë noted with satisfaction.

As long as that? Rico ground his jaw. Another reason to curse the fact he had stayed away too long. He couldn't let her go—he didn't want to let her go—and he wanted to find out what she was hiding. 'You don't know these mountains at night. This path is dangerous. There's a lot of loose stone, and plenty of sheer drops.'

'I'll take my chances.'

'The road isn't half bad.'

Somehow he managed to grace his last words with a smile. She stopped struggling and looked at him, her bright green eyes full of suspicion.

'Come on, Zoë, you know you don't really want to walk.' Charm again? New ground for him, admittedly, but well worth it if she agreed. If he took her back he could take a look around. He knew her name from somewhere—and not just from the television. But how did she affect him? Was she a threat? 'It's only a short drive in the Jeep.'

'OK,' Zoë said at last.

She was relieved she didn't have to walk back in the dark. But as Rico dug for his keys in the back pocket of his jeans she wondered if she was quite sane. If it hadn't been for Maria's reassurances she would never have agreed to anything so foolish. She didn't know a thing about Rico Cortes, and the day her divorce came through she had promised herself no more tough guys, no more being pushed around, mentally or physically.

'Don't look so worried. You'll be a lot safer going down

the mountain in the Jeep with me. Are you coming or not?'
he said when she still hesitated. 'I've got work tomorrow.'

'Tomorrow's Sunday.'

'That's right—and I have things to get ready for Monday
morning.'

'What things?' Maybe he *was* the local brigand, and
Monday was his day for mustering the troops. And she had
agreed to take a lift home with him...

Zoë frowned as he opened the passenger door for her. Rico
Cortes was as much a mystery now as ever, and it wasn't like
her. She was an expert at winkling out information. It was the
secret of her success—or had been in the past.

The moment he swung into the driver's seat beside her she
fired off another question. 'What keeps you in this part of
Spain?' He was larger than life, which went with the dramatic
scenery, but he didn't fit into the small-town scene at all.

'I have many interests.'

'Such as?'

He didn't answer as he gunned the engine into life. The
noise was supposed to distract her, she guessed. He was dodg-
ing her questions like an expert—almost as if he was used to
dealing with the media.

Local reporter, maybe?

No way! And better not to ask—better not to get involved.
She had only just won her freedom from an unhappy marriage. Divorce had come at a high price, even if the break had
been like a cleansing torrent that washed most of her insecurities away. And she didn't want them back again. Ever. So
why had she agreed to take a lift back to the castle with a
man she didn't know? The only answer was that Maria liked
him, and she liked Maria.

Was that enough? It had to be, Zoë realised as they pulled
away.

Maria had said he was a fighter. El Paladín. Was fighting

his profession? Zoë felt a quiver of apprehension run down her spine as she flashed a glance at him.

No, it couldn't be. Not unless he was the luckiest pugilist alive. He was built like a fighter but his face was unmarked, and his hands, as she had already noticed, were smooth. And in spite of his casual clothes, and his life up in this remote mountainous region, he had polish. But then quite a few boxers did too...

'Seen enough, Zoë?'

'I'm sorry, was I staring? I'm so tired I hardly know what I'm doing.'

Rico could feel the sexual tension between them rising fast. Any other time, any other woman, he might have swung off the road and fixed it for them both. But he had to know more about a woman before he got involved. He wasn't about to commit some reckless indiscretion Zoë Chapman could broadcast to the world.

He had learned not to court disaster on his own doorstep. She was luscious, but she would keep, and she backed off every time he looked at her. If she had kept her legs crossed all this time she would wait a little longer.

What if she was innocent? It seemed unlikely, but— No. Life wasn't like that. Fate never dealt him an easy hand.

Guilty, innocent—it hardly mattered which. He would still go slow until he'd worked out what made her tick... Go slow? So he *was* going somewhere with her?

Rico smiled. He could feel Zoë looking at him. Life got too easy at the top of the mountain. He hadn't had anything approaching a real challenge to deal with in quite some time.

Normally Zoë was a confident passenger, but Rico Cortes scared the hell out of her driving back down the steep track. He really did know the mountains like the back of his hand. And the speed he took the road, it was just as well—because the only faster way would have been over a cliff.

She was relieved to arrive back in one piece at the castle,

and even more relieved when she talked him out of staying. He'd wanted to look around, but he couldn't argue when she pointed out how late it was and that they would wake everyone up. But he would be back on Tuesday for the party—he made that clear.

This mess had to be sorted out before then.

Zoë groaned as she looked round the set. She had discussed the layout with her chief designer. But, according to the note she'd found propped up on the kitchen table, Carla had been called home to attend a family emergency and her young assistant had stepped in.

Zoë couldn't be angry with him; she could see he had tried. But he had fallen a long way short of achieving the authentic look she had decided on with Carla. How could she expect Maria to take part in a show that featured a fake Spanish kitchen decorated with imitation fruit? It might look real enough through a camera lens, but it would never pass close scrutiny, and it would only reinforce Rico's misconceptions about her work.

Why should he barge into her thoughts? She had more important things to consider—like rescuing the programme from disaster! Men like Rico Cortes were no good—great to drool over, maybe, but worse than lousy in real life.

Planting her hands on her hips, Zoë looked round again, but things didn't improve on closer inspection.

Posters brashly proclaiming the title of her latest bestselling cookery book were tacked up everywhere, while garish bunting was strung overhead. The exquisite marble-tiled floor had been hidden beneath a hideous orange carpet, and in the centre of the shag-pile the open-fronted area where she would be filmed sat in all its plywood and plastic glory. Hardly any attempt had been made to mask the fact that it was blatantly fake. There was lurid fake greenery draped around the top, with plastic fruit tacked in clumps to the backdrop.

It would all have to come down, but it could wait until the

morning. She couldn't concentrate while she was so tired. She couldn't concentrate while her thoughts kept straying back to Rico Cortes. A good night's sleep would help her get over him, and then she would get down to work.

As soon as it was light Zoë leapt out of bed. The crew were due on set at nine for a technical rehearsal. That was when the lights, camera angles and sound levels would be decided upon. The best she could hope for was that they would sleep in. She didn't have much time to strip the set and redress it, but it was important she had an authentic set in place for the rehearsal so there would be little or no change when she recorded the programme. She didn't like surprises when the red light went on.

Half an hour later she had picked fruit straight from the trees and brought in a basket full of greenery from the shady part of the castle gardens. Each time she'd visited the market in Cazulas Zoë hadn't been able to resist buying another piece of the local hand-painted pottery, and she now laid out her hoard on a working table along with the fresh produce.

She stared up at the plastic bunting.

Balancing halfway up a ladder wasn't easy, but, working quickly, she got the bunting down, then moved to the 'fishing net' on the back wall of the set to flip out some more tacks. Then she still had to tackle the plastic castanets pinned up with the plastic fruit on the same wall. Proper wooden castanets were miniature works of art. They came alive in the hands of an artist like Maria. These plastic efforts were about as Spanish as chop suey!

Sticking the screwdriver she had found in a kitchen drawer into the back pocket of her jeans, Zoë glanced at her wristwatch and made a swift calculation. If she could get the rest of them down without too much trouble, she might just finish in time.

'Talk about a relief!'

'Are you speaking to me?'

'Rico!' Zoë nearly fell off her ladder with shock. 'What are you doing here?' Her knuckles turned white as she gripped on tight. She watched transfixed as he swooped on the clutch of castanets she had just dropped to the floor.

'Very nice,' he said, examining them. 'Which region of Spain do these represent?'

'Bargain basement,' Zoë tried lightly, trying to regulate her breathing at the same time. How could any man look so good so early in the morning after hardly any sleep? It just wasn't human. 'How did you get in?' she said, as it suddenly struck her that she would never have gone to bed and left the front door wide open.

He ignored her question—and her attempted humour. 'What is all this rubbish?'

Coming down the ladder as quickly as she could in safety, Zoë faced him. 'The set for my television show.' Her appreciative mood was evaporating rapidly. She had never seen such scorn on anyone's face.

'I gathered that.' He stared around with disapproval.

OK, so it was a mess—but it was her mess, and she would sort it out. Zoë could feel her temper rising. According to the lease, at this moment Castillo Cazulas belonged to her. She could do with it what she liked. And if plastic castanets were her style, Señor Testosterone would just have to put up with it.

Reaching out, she took them from him. 'Thank you.' His hands felt warm and dry. They felt great. 'Can I help you with anything?' Her voice was cool, but she was trembling inside.

'Yes, you can. You can get all this trash out of here.'

'Trash?'

'You heard me. I want it all removed.'

'Oh, you do?' Zoë said, meeting his stare. 'And what business is it of yours, exactly?'

Ignoring her question, Rico paced the length of the set, shoulders hunched, looking like a cold-eyed panther stalking its prey. 'You can't seriously expect an artist of Maria's calibre to perform in this *theme park*?'

'No, of course I don't—'

'Then get all this down! Get rid of it! Do whatever you have to do to put it right—just don't let me see it the next time I'm here.'

'Next time? There doesn't have to be a next time, Rico,' Zoë assured him with a short, humourless laugh.

'Oh, forgive me.' He came closer. 'I thought you invited me here for Tuesday.'

'If you feel so bad about all this—' Zoë opened her arms wide '—there's an easy solution.'

'Oh?'

'I'll just withdraw my invitation, and then you won't have to suffer another moment's distress.'

'That would be too easy for you.'

'Easy?' Zoë rested one hand on her head and stared at him incredulously. What the hell was easy about any of this? As far as she was concerned, nothing had been easy since she'd run up against Rico Cortes.

'If you want Maria to dance, I'll be here.'

'Oh, I see,' Zoë said sarcastically. 'You own Maria. You make all her decisions for her—'

'Don't be so ridiculous.'

'So what do you think is going to happen here, Rico? As far as I know we'll be making a television programme. I'll be cooking, Maria will dance, and everyone in the village will have a great time at the party. Is that so terrible?'

He made a contemptuous sound. 'You make it sound so straightforward.'

'Because it is!' What was he getting at? Why didn't he trust her?

They glared at each other without blinking, and then Rico

broke away to stare around. His expression hardened. 'You don't seriously expect me to allow my friends to come to a place like this on Tuesday night.'

'Oh, so now you own the whole village? I didn't realise the feudal system was alive and well in Cazulas. I suppose it's never occurred to you that my neighbours might be capable of thinking for themselves?'

'Your neighbours don't know what you plan to do here.'

'What *do* I plan to do, exactly?'

'You don't respect them.'

'How do you know that?'

'You don't respect their culture.'

'How dare you say that?'

'How dare I?' Rico's voice was contemptuous as he glared down at her.

He was close enough for her to touch—or attack—but she would never lower herself to that. She wasn't about to lose control, like every man she had ever known, and let Rico add that to her long list of shortcomings.

'You come here to Cazulas—Cazulas, of all the flamenco villages in Spain! And you try to tell me it's just a coincidence? And then you bring Maria into it. Another coincidence? I don't think so.'

She'd had enough. She wasn't going to stand by and let him rant. 'You're right, Rico. Bringing Maria into my plans was no coincidence. The reason I asked her to appear on my programme is because she is easily the best dancer I have ever seen. She is certainly the best performer in Cazulas. That's no coincidence; it's a fact.' Zoë couldn't be sure if Rico had heard her or not. He was so tense, so angry—like a wound-up spring on the point of release.

'You come here with your television cameras and your questions.' He gazed around the half-finished set contemptuously. 'You throw together some cheap items and pass it off as a Spanish setting. You really think that's going to convince me that you're putting together some worthy programme about cultural influences on Spanish cooking? You must think I'm stupid.'

'You're certainly mistaken.' But she could see that he might think she was putting up the plastic rubbish, rather than taking it down.

He was so still, so keyed up, he reminded her of a big cat before it pounced. Zoë was beginning to ache with holding herself so stiffly. She sagged with relief when he pulled away from her with a jerk.

'I'll be back to check up on you later. If this rubbish isn't removed by then you can forget Tuesday. Maria will not be dancing for you.'

'Doesn't Maria have a mind of her own?'

Rico was already striding towards the door. He stopped dead. He couldn't believe that she would still dare to challenge him. 'Yes, of course Maria has a mind of her own. She will take one look at this mess and refuse to dance.'

'Oh, get out!'

As he wheeled around he saw the local produce—fresh fruit, greenery, even some attractive pieces of hand-painted pottery. His lips curled in a sneer of contempt. Someone had planned to do something classy for the programme, something appropriate to the area. What a shame Zoë Chapman didn't have any taste.

She really was no better than the rest. Even if she didn't work at the gutter end of television, he would not stand by and see her discard Maria the moment her usefulness was at an end. Maria was too soft-hearted for her own good. It was up to him to protect her from people like Zoë Chapman.

Zoë jumped as the door slammed. Contempt for the disastrous set was about where her dial was pointing, too. But that didn't give Rico Cortes the right to come storming in, ordering her about.

Snatching a plastic parrot down from his perch, she tossed

it into the bin bag with the rest of the rubbish. She hated being caught on the back foot, hated leaving Rico Cortes with the impression that this was all her doing. Most of all she hated the fact that he was coming back to check up on her later. Who the hell did he think he was?

But it would have been far worse still if he hadn't planned to come back at all.

CHAPTER THREE

IT WAS all Rico could do to stay away from the castle. It was barely noon. He had planned to return around late afternoon, but every moment since leaving the castle had been torture.

He had never witnessed such desecration in his life. That was the only reason he was pressing his heel to the floor now. He ground his jaw with satisfaction as the Jeep surged forward. Zoë wouldn't expect him until later, and a surprise visit always revealed more than a planned return. With any luck he would catch her unawares.

Maybe she wasn't the type of tabloid journalist he loathed, but she was still as shallow as the rest, still ignorant of the precious heritage Maria carried forward in the village.

Before he'd left the castle that morning he'd found a member of the television crew, who had assured him they would still be in rehearsal at midday. The youth had also confessed that he was responsible for the set design.

What type of television company used boys fresh out of college for such responsible work? If she owned a decent television company, why didn't she have a proper set designer? Plastic parrots! What the hell did she think she was filming? *Treasure Island?* And what kind of programme had sets dressed with garish rubbish? He could think of a few cable channels that might have gone down that route, and none of them was respectable.

He'd seen Zoë up a ladder dressed in figure-hugging jeans and a skimpy top, instead of her shapeless track suit—and he'd heard her harangue him. He knew now she could play angel or vamp with equal zest.

Glancing at his watch, Rico smiled grimly. He had timed

it just right. The rehearsal should have started. He would check out what line of entertainment Zoë Chapman was really in. Anticipation surged through him. Even through the red mist of his rage this morning she'd looked sensational. Pin-thin women weren't his style, and there was nothing pin-like about Ms Chapman. What would she wear to play her plastic castanets? She had curves that would have done credit to a Rubens.

Slowing the Jeep as he approached the ancient stonework, Rico picked up speed as he hit the long main drive. Accelerating down the avenue of cypress trees, he gave a final spin of the wheel and turned into the familiar cobbled court-yard.

Leaning back with his arms folded against a door at the far end of the Great Hall, he didn't announce his presence, just stood watching in silence. No one noticed him in the shadows. All the focus was on Zoë, in front of the camera.

Even he had to admit the transformation to the set was marked. In place of the fairground bunting and fake castanets there was a plain wooden butcher's block upon which she appeared to be chopping a mountain of herbs. She had a collection of wine bottles at her side, and from their shape he recognised a couple as coming from pretty decent cellars.

Rico began to feel increasingly uncomfortable as he watched Zoë working—and he never felt uncomfortable. But then, he had never misjudged anyone quite so badly before.

She couldn't possibly have thrown all this together in a few minutes. It had to be how she always worked—she was too familiar with everything around her for it to be a sham. Brass pots gleamed brightly on the cooking range, and the imple-ments suspended from an overhead rail were all steel, with not a single gimmick in sight. There were wooden bowls close to hand on the counter where she was working, as well as several white porcelain saucers—bearing a selection of spices, he supposed. Next to them a large, shallow blue and white ceramic bowl overflowed with fresh vegetables. Maybe there were a lot of other things he couldn't trust about her, but this was real enough. He had to give her credit for that.

Zoë worked quickly and deftly, her small hands moving instinctively about the necessary tasks as she addressed herself cheerfully to camera. She had charisma as well as beauty, Rico thought, and he felt a sudden longing to harness her smiles and turn them in his own direction.

But how was he supposed to believe she had turned up in Cazulas by chance? If he could talk her into having dinner with him, maybe he could find out. But it wouldn't be easy after their ill-tempered exchange that morning... Easing away from the door, he decided to go. He had seen all he needed to see.

In between takes, Zoë's glance kept straying to the door. Half of her wanted to see Rico again, while the other half dreaded him walking in unannounced. But she needn't have worried because her director, Philip, had just wrapped the day's filming and there was still no sign of Rico. Empty threats, Zoë presumed. Rico's Spanish pride had taken a hit when she'd stood up to him. Or maybe she was just beneath contempt. That was probably it. His face when he'd seen the apprentice set designer's attempts to recreate a 'typical' Spanish setting had said it all. He'd thought she meant to trivialise everything he held dear.

And what was the point of trying to explain when he never listened? But he might have let her know if the others still planned to come on Tuesday night. If he had put them off... She would have to make sure he hadn't talked Maria out of appearing on the programme or she would be facing disaster. Perhaps she should go back to the mountains and find out what was happening?

Zoë was still frowning when one of the girls in the crew asked if she would like to eat with them in the local café that

evening. 'I'd really love to come with you,' she said honestly,
'but there's something else I have to do first.'

Was all this totally necessary for a trek into the mountains?
Zoë asked herself wryly as she craned her neck to check her
rear view in the elegant console mirror. Of course she could
always take off the snug-fitting jeans and replace them with
a dirndl skirt... *No way!* And what about the blouse: ever so
slightly see-through, with just one too many buttons left undone? OK, so maybe that was going a step too far. She fas-
tened it almost to the neck. Reaching for a lightweight cotton
sweater from the chair, she checked her hair one last time and
then added a slick of lipgloss and a spritz of perfume.

Her eyes were glittering like aquamarine in a face that
seemed unusually pale, Zoë noticed—apart from two smudges
of red, high on each cheekbone. That was thanks to excitement at finally bringing the programme together. It was the
culmination of a year of hard work. It had nothing at all to
do with the fact that she might be seeing Rico Cortes again.

She had come to him. Rico subdued the rush of triumph before it had time to register on his face. 'Ms Chapman,' he
said coolly. 'To what do we owe this pleasure?'

Leaning back against a gnarled tree trunk, arms folded, he
watched Zoë's approach through narrowed eyes. Her unaf-
fected grace was so like that of the dancers she admired, and
she looked great in casual clothes. She wore little make-up,
and her skin was honey-gold from her time in the sun. She
was beautiful—very different from the glamorous women he
was used to outside Cazulas, but all the more beautiful for
that. The light was slipping away fast, and the sky behind the
snow-capped mountains was more dramatic than any he had
seen for a while: a radiant banner of violet and tangerine—
the perfect backdrop for their latest encounter. The night

breeze was kicking up, rustling through the leaves above his head as she walked up to him.

'You said you would come back to the castle.'

Her blunt statement took him by surprise—a pleasant one. 'I did come back, but you were working.'

That rather took the wind out of her sails, Zoë thought, but her heart was still thumping so violently she felt sure Rico would be able to hear it. 'I see.' She was relieved to sound so cool. 'I trust the changes I made met with your exacting standards?'

He gave a short laugh and relaxed. 'You did a great job, Zoë. Can I get you a drink?'

'Nothing stronger than orange juice!'

'Fine by me.'

He gestured that she should follow him, and his impressive rear view led her to silently praise the inventor of close-fitting jeans.

It was too early for the campfire to be lit, but there were still quite a lot of people around. Most of them were waiting for the children to finish their dance class. This meeting place served a number of functions, Zoë realised. There was the social side, and the performance opportunities, as well as the very valuable teaching that went on to preserve tradition.

She could see the youngsters now, tense with excitement and anticipation as they clustered around their dance teacher, listening to what she had to say. In another area a couple of the boys were sitting at the feet of the guitarist who had played for Maria, watching engrossed as his agile fingers rippled across the strings.

Pouring them both some juice from a covered jug that had been left for the children on a trestle table, Rico handed a glass to Zoë and then took her to sit with him on a flat rock out of the way. Crossing one leg over the other, he rested his chin on his hand as he listened to the music.

The low, insistent rhythm of the solo guitar was the perfect

soundtrack for Rico Cortes, Zoë thought, glancing at him sur-
reptitiously as she sipped her drink. Dressed in simple black
jeans and a black top, he made her heart judder, he looked so
good. The close-fitting top defined every muscle and sinew
across the wide spread of his shoulders, and the jeans moulded
thighs powerful enough to control a wild stallion, or a
woman…

'You're far too early to see any of the adult performers
dance, you know,' he said, his gaze lingering on Zoë's face
as the guitarist picked out a particularly plangent arpeggio.

'I haven't come to see them,' she said, meeting his gaze
steadily.

'Oh?' A crooked smile tugged at one corner of his mouth.

'Or you,' she said immediately. 'I hoped I might find
Maria.'

'Well, you will—but you can't talk to her yet. So you might
just as well settle back and enjoy the children rehearsing for
our fiesta.'

'Fiesta? That must be fun.' Zoë turned to watch them.
'Does everyone take part in the fiesta?'

'Why don't you come along and see for yourself?'

She wanted to. She really wanted to feel part of Cazulas.
Since the moment she'd arrived in the village she had felt an
affinity with the area, and with the people. Rico made it sound
so easy for her to become part of their way of life, but she
wouldn't be staying that long.

'When will everyone else arrive?' Zoë looked around.
There were a few cars parked already, notably Rico's rugged
black Jeep.

'Most people take a long, lazy siesta in the afternoon, when
the weather gets hot.'

'So Maria's still in bed?' Zoë could feel the blood rushing
to her cheeks. Where was she going with *this* line of ques-
tioning?

'Many people are still in bed—but Maria is not one of

them.' Standing up, he beckoned to Zoë to follow him, and, walking ahead of her, he made for the stage where the children were still learning their steps.

Once again, he reminded Zoë of a big black panther. He had the same grace and stealth of a big cat, and made her feel very small by comparison. It was impossible not to imagine how it might feel to be enclosed in his arms and held safe. Or to be pinned down by those long, hard-muscled legs, and— *Stop it! Stop it now!* This was dangerous.

'Zoë?'

'Maria!' Zoë exclaimed, throwing her brain into gear. 'I'm sorry, I was daydreaming. I didn't realise it was you dancing with the children. It's good to see you again.'

'Why have you come here? Not to see the children, I think,' Maria said, tapping the side of her nose.

'No—no, of course not,' Zoë said, recovering fast. 'I came to see you.'

'Ah,' Maria said, staring at her keenly.

'I wanted to make sure you hadn't changed your mind.'

'Changed my mind? About dancing on Tuesday, you mean?' Maria said. 'Why would I?'

'Oh, I don't know,' Zoë said, suddenly embarrassed at the weakness of her supposed mission. She was conscious of Rico watching them, arms folded, with the same brooding look that made her quiver. 'I just wanted to be sure no one had put you off the idea.' She stopped, thinking frantically for something to explain her visit. 'After all, you don't know me—'

'Stop worrying,' Maria insisted. 'I will be there for you on Tuesday, Zoë. Your television programme will be made, and everything will turn out for the best in the end.'

Would it? Zoë wondered. There were moments when she wished she had never come to Spain. A fresh start was supposed to be just that—not a rerun with a matching set of characters that just happened to have different names.

Was she overreacting? She really hoped so. Men like Rico

had always been her downfall: big, powerful men like her ex-husband. Men who oozed testosterone through every pore; men who made her believe she could be desirable and might even find sexual fulfilment with them.

Unconsciously, Zoë made a small sound of despair. She was a sexual oddity—and likely to remain so. She was frightened of sex, it always hurt, and she wasn't sure how to improve the situation. Her husband had grown tired of her excuses. She had made him hate her. Small wonder they had divorced.

But that was behind her now. She had rebuilt her life. She couldn't allow anyone, especially Rico Cortes, to fan her past insecurities into flame...

'Zoë?' Maria asked softly. 'What is the matter?'

'Nothing.' Collecting herself, Zoë spoke firmly and smiled. 'Now,' she added quickly, before Maria could probe any deeper, 'I'd like to discuss my outline plan for the programme in which you're to appear. I want to be quite sure you're happy with everything.'

'*Bueno,*' Maria murmured softly, frowning a little as she allowed Zoë to lead her away from Rico.

The two women remained deep in conversation for some time. They were both on the same wavelength, Zoë realised. Maria was only too pleased to have the opportunity to bring genuine Spanish culture to a wider audience, and Zoë liked to present her food in context, rather than offering individual, unconnected recipes. This was her definition of lifestyle TV— a show that was genuine in every single respect—and now she had control over the content of her own programmes it was exactly what she delivered.

It was going to be really good, she realised with a sudden rush of excitement. Maria's talent would imbue the show with her own special quality. Rico had correctly identified it as something that no amount of money could buy.

Glancing around, Zoë looked for him. But he must have left while she was talking to Maria.

'Don't look so sad,' Maria insisted, chucking her under the chin. 'I know what we will do,' she added, getting to her feet.

Once again Zoë was struck by the difference in mobility between the Maria who had been sitting next to her and the Maria who performed on the stage—the one so fluid and graceful, the other showing definite, if gracious, signs of her age. 'What will we do, Maria?'

'We will dance together.'

'Oh, no, I can't—'

'You can walk, you can run, and you can jump?'

'Well, yes, of course—'

'Then you can dance,' Maria told her sternly. 'But first we must find you some clothes. Those will not do,' she said, eyeing Zoë's slim-fitting jeans and top. 'You look like a boy. I want to make you look like a woman.'

Zoë's eyes widened. She was too polite to argue. And far too curious to see what Maria meant to refuse.

Now she knew the secret of the wooden mountain house around which people congregated. It was packed to the rafters with the most spectacular clothes: rows of shoes, boxes of hair ornaments, cascading fringed shawls, and dresses by the score in every colour under the rainbow.

'You're so lucky to take performing under the stars for granted.' Zoë peered out of one of the small windows at the darkening sky. Someone had lit the campfire, and flames were just beginning to take hold. It was such a romantic scene, like something out of an old musical film. The children were still rehearsing—not because they had to now, but because they wanted to. Their heads were held high, faces rapt, their backs were arched and their hands expressive. 'The children are a credit to you, Maria.'

Maria paused as she sorted through the dresses packed tight

on the rail. 'They are a credit to themselves and to each other,' she corrected Zoë gently. 'And if they can do it, so can you.'

'Oh, no, really—I can't—' Her dancing was confined to her classes.

'Who said you can't? Here, try these on.'

Maria brought her an armful of clothes and Zoë's face broke into a smile. Maria was like a gust of fresh spring air behind a heavy rain cloud. It was impossible to be hooked by the past when she was around.

'The colour of this dress will look good on you.'

Zoë exclaimed with pleasure as she gazed at the beautiful lilac dress. Maria's confidence was infectious.

'You can put the dress on over there.' Maria pointed across the room. 'That's where the children get changed—behind that screen. When you have it on, come out and choose some shoes to fit you from this row here. Don't worry—I will help you to finish fastening the dress, and then I will do your hair.'

For once it was a pleasure to do as she was told. Zoë knew she would dance, because Maria would give her the confidence to do so. She was excited at the prospect of trying something new, especially now Rico had gone. She wouldn't have wanted to make a show of herself if he'd still been around.

Maria was right; the low-cut lilac dress did look good against her titian hair. It moulded her figure like a glove down to her hips, where it flared out, and then was longer at one side than the other. She was showing quite a bit of leg, Zoë saw in the mirror, raising the skirt with a flourish. Just wearing the dress made her stand straight and proud, made her want to toss back her hair with the same defiant move she had seen Maria perform on stage.

Dipping her chin, Zoë tried out her expression, staring fiercely into the mirror through a fringe of long lashes. A poster on the wall behind her caught her attention. The dark-haired young woman was incredibly beautiful. Passion blazed from her eyes as she glared straight into the camera. She had the sinuous frame of a top model, though was more striking than any model Zoë had ever seen. Her full lips were slightly parted and a strand of her long ebony hair had caught across them, giving her flamenco pose a sense of movement. There was a single word stretched across the top of the fiery background: Beba.

'*Bueno!*' Maria said with approval when Zoë finally emerged from behind the screen. 'That dress really suits you. I knew it would. Let me just finish the hooks and eyes at the back for you. They are hard for you to reach.'

'I feel different. It's ridiculous, but—'

'It's flamenco.' Maria laughed happily and stood back to look at Zoë. 'Now you feel proud and confident, like a woman should. Come, I will arrange your hair for you. And then we dance!'

Taka taka taka tak tak tak…taka taka taka tak… She was doing it! They had practised for about an hour on the dusty ground, and now Maria had deemed Zoë ready for the stage where, working together, the heels of their shoes made a crisp, satisfying sound on the hard wooden floor.

Breathing hard, her face fierce with concentration, Zoë thrust her head back as Maria had directed. One arm sweeping behind her back, she raised the other hand stiff, in a defiant pose, as if calling up some invisible energy…

'*Olé!*'

'Rico!'

'Don't stop now,' Maria ordered sharply.

But Zoë suddenly felt exposed and foolish. 'I'd much rather watch you,' she said, moving to the back of the stage. 'You haven't danced a solo yet.'

'I'm saving myself,' Maria said sardonically. 'Whereas you, Zoë, are hiding yourself.'

'That's not true…'

'Isn't it?' Maria demanded as Rico approached the stage.

'Why did you stop?' He stared up at Zoë.

'I'm very much a beginner—I'm not ready to perform in public.' Her heart lurched at his assessing look.

'But from what I have seen you have potential—don't you agree, Maria?'

'*Mucho* potential,' Maria agreed, but she made a disapproving sound with her tongue against the roof of her mouth when she looked at Rico, as if she sensed some double meaning behind his words.

'So, will you dance for me, Zoë?'

Rico's question had an alarming effect on Zoë's senses. It was like every seduction technique imaginable condensed into a few short words. She would love nothing more than to dance for him, with this new and abandoned feeling rushing through her. Just the thought of being so uninhibited in his presence was tempting. She felt strong, and in control, and highly sexual—as if the dance had enabled her to plunge head first into a world of sensuality for the first time in her life. Sucking in a deep, shuddering breath, Zoë realised she loved the feeling. It was intoxicating—and extremely dangerous.

'I'm waiting for your answer,' Rico reminded her.

Zoë glanced around, but Maria had melted away, lost in the crowds already gathering for that night's performance.

'Come down from there.'

She looked at him and hesitated.

'Please, Zoë?'

She was surprised. His voice had gentled.

'I don't bite, and—'

'Are you apologising to me?' Zoë said, cocking her head to one side as she looked at him.

'Me?' Rico half smiled at her as he touched one hand to his chest.

His eyes were different now, she noticed. Darker, still a

little guarded, but warmer—definitely warmer. 'Yes, you. Who else has doubted my motives in Cazulas, Rico?'

And he still doubted her motives. But he could handle it. He could handle her too. 'So, you're too timid to dance for me?'

'I don't do private exhibitions.'

'That's a pity.'

'Is it? Would you really think more of me if I made a habit of dancing for men? I don't think so. You've already shown your contempt for me—I can just imagine what you would make of that.'

'I admit we've got off to a bad start—'

'That's putting it mildly.'

'So, here's our chance to start again.'

'Should I want to?'

She saw his mouth quirk at one corner, as if he wanted to smile.

'I hoped you might.'

Zoë half turned away, lifting her chin as she considered his words. 'I'm not so sure,' she said, turning back to him again with a frown. 'Why should I? I don't need the aggravation.'

'Who said anything about aggravation, Zoë? Come on— come down from there and let's talk.'

She couldn't stand up on the stage all night. People were beginning to stare at her. She would have to do something soon—dance a solo or get off the stage. Picking up her skirt, she walked briskly down the steps.

'Zoë, please.'

She looked down at Rico's hand on her arm. 'This had better be good.'

'I hope you think so.'

She gasped when he drew her in front of him. 'Rico, what—?'

'I think I've behaved rather badly.'

'Yes, you have.' It was harder than she had thought to meet his gaze this close up.

'I can understand why you don't feel like trusting me now.'

'Can you?' She didn't trust herself either when he was around.

'Will you let me make amends? Have dinner with me.'

Zoë stared at him. Was he serious?

'Zoë?'

She had to get herself out of this somehow. 'I've got an idea.'

'Which is?'

He seemed amused. But hopefully this would get her off the hook. It was the only challenge she could think of that Rico wouldn't want to take up. 'If you cook for me, I'll dance for you.'

'*Bueno.*' He didn't waste any time over his answer. 'Shall we say later tonight?'

'Tonight?' All the breath seemed suddenly to have been sucked out of her lungs.

'We eat late in Spain.' Rico was quite matter-of-fact about it. Did he think her hesitation was due to ignorance of local customs? 'Shall we say ten o'clock?'

'Ten o'clock?' Zoë repeated, staring up at him blankly.

'Yes, let's say ten. That will give you enough time to prepare.'

To prepare what? She bit her lip. Unaccountably, her brain stalled, and not a single word of refusal made it to her lips.

'Then it's agreed,' Rico said with satisfaction. 'We will meet again, later tonight, at Castillo Cazulas.'

CHAPTER FOUR

THIS was the last thing she had expected to be doing, Zoë thought, as she tested the small four-wheel drive she had just hired to its limits. Rico had said he would follow her back to the castle later, to cook the meal and watch her dancing. She could only hope he was joking. The idea of dancing for him already seemed ridiculous.

Glancing in the driver's mirror, she saw the bundle of clothes Maria had insisted she take with her, assuring her that she would feel more comfortable dancing in them than jeans. More comfortable? Maybe—until Rico saw her wearing the flimsy low-necked blouse and ultra-feminine practice skirt!

She knew she was playing with fire, but where Rico Cortes was concerned it seemed she couldn't resist courting danger. Fortunately the film crew would be out partying until late, so no one would even know what she planned to do—or what kind of fool she made of herself.

As she pulled into the courtyard she thought about cancelling. But she didn't know how to get hold of Rico—and why should she pull out? She was more likely to dance than he was to cook. It was an opportunity to redress the balance between them...he would never doubt her will again.

The heavy iron knocker echoed ominously through the long stone passages as Zoë hurried to open the front door. Prompt at ten o'clock, Rico had said, and he was bang on time, she saw, glancing up at the tall grandfather clock on the turn of the stairs.

She was shivering all over with excitement and apprehension, and, reaching the hallway, she made herself slow down. She didn't want to appear too keen.

But as she walked her hips swayed beneath the ankle-length skirt, and as the swathes of fabric brushed her naked legs she knew the clothes Maria had given her to wear made her move quite differently. Even the simple peasant blouse was enough to make her want to throw her head back and walk tall. No wonder the women of Spain looked so magnificent when they stepped onto a stage when all their clothes were designed to make the most of the female form.

'Zoë.'

She could feel her face heating up as Rico stared at her. She tried for cool and unconcerned as she stood aside to let him pass. 'Welcome. How nice to see you.'

Nice! Zoë felt as if a furnace had just roared into flame somewhere inside her. She felt weak, she felt strong, and her legs were trembling uncontrollably beneath her skirt. She registered the flash of a dark, imperious gaze, and then he was gone, walking past her towards the kitchen.

He seemed to know his way—but then he would. Who knew how long he had been hanging around the castle earlier that morning? And so far he seemed to be keeping his side of the bargain: he had a box of provisions, as well as a guitar case slung over his shoulder.

'That was absolutely delicious,' she said, some time later.

'You seem surprised.'

She was, Zoë realised. Not only had Rico kept to his part of their bargain, he was an excellent cook. 'I am.'

'Because I can cook?'

Zoë smiled. It was hard to concentrate on anything apart from Rico's face as he stared at her. It wiped her mind clean, made her long to know him better. Physically, he was everything she knew to avoid. But they were alone together, and she wondered if she had misjudged him. He was still proud, male and alpha, but he had a sense of humour too—something she hadn't anticipated. 'I'm not surprised you can cook. I'm just surprised that you can cook so well.'

'Is there any reason why I should be incapable of feeding myself?'

'Of course not. It's just that most men—'

'Most men?'

She loved the way one of his eyebrows tilted a fraction when he asked a question. She'd been thinking of her ex, sitting at the table waiting for his meal after they had both put in a long day at work. He'd only commented on her food when it hadn't been to his liking. She had never received a compliment from him for her cooking.

'Most men wouldn't know their way around a warm barbecued vegetable salad with anchovies.'

'Escalivada amb anxoves?' Rico translated for her. 'It's a great dish, isn't it? My mother is a fabulous cook, and she taught all her children how to prepare food. It is no big deal.' He got to his feet to collect their plates.

'Your mother?' Instantly Zoë was curious. Either Rico ignored her interest, or he didn't notice. But she noticed the fact that he was clearing up after them. He wouldn't even allow her to help, just pushed her gently back down in her chair again.

'Save your strength for the dancing.'

His eyes were glinting with humour again. Not mockery, humour—humour shared between them. Feeling her confidence returning, Zoë smiled back. 'You know your way round a dishwasher too. I'm impressed.'

'You must have known some very strange men in your time, Zoë.'

Zoë smiled faintly. *You don't want to know how strange.*

Rico insisted on doing everything—even wiping down the surfaces and clearing the condiments from the table. Only when the kitchen had been returned to its former pristine condition did he turn to her.

'Now it is time for you to dance, Zoë.'

His eyes, she noticed, were already dancing—with laughter and with challenge. But somehow it gave her courage. He gave her courage.

'I'm ready. After that meal I've got a lot to live up to, so I'd better limber up before I begin. I would hate to disappoint you.'

'I will tune my guitar while you prepare.'

How long would that take? she wondered. Not long enough for her to be ready to dance for him, that was for sure!

As fast as Zoë's courage had returned, it vanished again. She wanted to impress Rico, and doubted she could. She wanted his gaze to linger on her, to bathe her in his admiration. She wanted him to want her as much as she wanted him.

She wanted to know more about his mother, Zoë corrected herself fiercely.

'Why don't we have pudding first, and talk a little longer?'

'You can't put it off all night. Are you having second thoughts, Zoë?'

'Not at all.'

'Then no more delaying tactics,' Rico said, reaching for his guitar. 'Sweet things come later, when we have earned them.'

How good his command of English was! His few words had set her on fire. She hadn't given a moment's thought to *later*, but clearly Rico had.

Subduing a rush of apprehension, Zoë led the way into the Great Hall. Rico sat on the stool she had placed there for him, and began adjusting the strings of his guitar.

'You have a beautiful guitar.' Under Rico's hands it had come to life, producing sounds that were rich and lovely.

'It's a flamenco guitar, made of spruce and cypress.'

'So it really does represent the music of the region?'

'Absolutely,' he murmured.

Zoë looked away first.

While Rico strummed some chords, testing them for clarity and tuning, Zoë centred herself, bending and stretching before the dance began.

Rico seemed to sense when she was ready to begin, and turned his head. With a brief nod, she walked to the centre of her improvised performance space in the centre of the vast square hall.

At first she was stiff and self-conscious, but Rico second-guessed her every move. She had never danced with such a sympathetic accompanist before—in fact she'd never danced with a real live accompanist before, and certainly not one who made her thrill even more than the music.

Rico made no allowances for the fact that she was new to flamenco, and in truth she didn't want him to; after just a short time she didn't need him to. Their partnership was as tight as Zoë could have wished, and after a few minutes all her tension disappeared.

There were some large ornate mirrors in this part of the hall, which was why she had chosen it. She could see Rico sitting cross-legged on his stool. He appeared lost in the music, but then he looked up and Zoë was lost in his eyes.

Instead of hesitating, Rico picked up the pace, his gaze boring into her as he drew rhythms hotter and more powerful than Zoë had ever thought possible from his guitar. His fingers moved at speed across the fretboard, producing an earthy sound that throbbed insistently through her. She could feel herself growing more abandoned with every step, until she was whirling in time to a rhythm of Rico's choosing. Then, abruptly, he slowed the tempo so that it rose and fell in waves of sound that dropped at last to a low and insistent rumble.

The sound was so faint Zoë could barely hear it. She might not have known he was still playing had it not been for the fact that she could still feel the music in every fibre of her being.

'That's enough for tonight,' he said suddenly, damping the strings with his hand.

She had been so absorbed in the dance, so lost in the sound he was creating, it took her a moment to come round and realise that Rico had stopped playing. She watched him prop his guitar against the wall, and was still in a sort of trance when he walked across the floor to her.

And then she came to with a bump, realising she was so aroused that her nipples were pressing tautly against the fine lawn top. Instinctively she lifted her hands to cover herself, but she could do nothing about the insistent pulse down low in her belly.

'I think you enjoyed that, Ms Chapman...and you're very good.' He stopped a few feet away, and made no attempt to close the gap.

Zoë licked her lips. Rico knew she was aroused. She could feel his response to that arousal enveloping her. He might as well have undone the ties on her blouse and exposed her erect nipples. Or lifted her skirt high above her waist and seen her there... He could arouse her as easily as that—without even touching her. And now she didn't want him to stop or turn away. This could be her one and only chance to push past arousal and see if she could handle the next stage...

'I think it's time for our dessert, Zoë.'

Zoë tried to hide her disappointment when Rico held out his hand to her. Her face was on fire at the thought she had made such a fool of herself. 'Dessert? Yes, of course.'

'Spanish-style.'

She saw the look in his eyes and felt a rush of heat flood through her as she realised that the last thing on Rico's mind was a return visit to the kitchen. *Oh.*

Her gaze fixed on his hand. He was waiting for her to clasp it. Was this what she wanted? Could she go ahead with it? Wasn't it better to stop now, before she proved to herself as well as Rico that as far as sex went she was one big disaster area? She didn't want to spoil the evening—which was what would happen if she allowed things to go any further.

For some reason the young flamenco dancer on the poster in the mountain hut flew into Zoë's mind. Beba was a proper woman, a sexual woman... But then Rico's arms closed around her and it was too late.

Zoë shuddered with desire as his mouth brushed her lips. She felt so small, so dainty—and desired. This far was fine— it was as far as she could ever go: a kiss, a light caress... She closed her eyes as he applied a little more pressure, his firm lips moving over her mouth until she softened against him.

Could so much pleasure come from a simple kiss? But there was nothing uncomplicated where Rico was concerned.

He felt her tense, and stroked her back with long, light strokes until she eased into him again. He tugged lightly with his teeth on her bottom lip until the tremors rippling through her reached her womb. She whimpered, wanting more, and, teasing her lips apart, he deepened the kiss.

Zoë accepted the pace Rico set just as she had accepted the music he had played for her—music that had begun so gently, so calmly... It was like that now. He was so strong she could sense the powerhouse contained beneath his tracing fingers and wonderfully caressing hands. His touch was as light as the softest chord on the guitar, and as if she was his instrument now the vibrations through her body went on and on.

As their kisses grew more heated she was swept up in the need to rub against him, to feel the hard bristle on his face scoring her cheeks, rasping her neck. Their breathing was hectic and there were sounds welling from deep inside their throats as the pace quickened like the fiery rhythms of flamenco. Need was overwhelming them. They were as rough now, and as mindlessly passionate, as the final furious torrent of demanding chords.

Then a flash of reality intruded, brutal and strong. She didn't know if she could stop him. He frightened her. She frightened herself. Things were getting out of control. What the hell was she doing?

Zoë tensed as the floodgates of the past gave way beneath the weight of ugly memories. 'No, no! Stop it! I can't—' She tried desperately to push him away.

'What do you mean, you can't?' Rico said sharply, holding her fast as he stared intently into her eyes.

'I just can't,' Zoë said, snatching her face away from his as she struggled to break free.

But he wouldn't let her go, and, cupping her chin, brought her back to face him again. 'What can't you do, Zoë? Answer me.'

She knew he sensed her fear.

'Tell me, please.'

His voice was gentle, and when she looked up at him their faces were almost touching.

'Tell me what's wrong, Zoë. Is there someone else?'

'I can't tell you what's wrong.' Zoë pressed her lips together. That was true. How could she? Where were the words to explain how some giant switch had simply turned off inside her, so that all she felt now with him was fear and apprehension?

'Has someone hurt you? Or do you already have a man? Did he do something to you? Did he hurt you?'

'No!' Zoë covered her ears with her hands, protecting herself against the barrage of questions, trying to shut out the ugly scenes replaying in her mind. She wasn't ready for this. Would she ever be ready?

But none of it was Rico's fault. Her gaze flew to his face, and she knew he saw the answer in her eyes.

'Zoë…Zoë.' He brought her close. 'Why didn't you tell me?'

'We don't know each other.' Her voice was muffled against his chest.

'I'd like to change that.'

She wanted to believe him. She wanted desperately to believe him, to think he might be different. But her past kept on insisting she was wrong. 'Can we change the subject?' She straightened her hair. 'What about if I make the pudding?'

'Zoë—'

'I don't mind.'

'Stop it, Zoë.' Pulling back, Rico held her in front of him.

'It won't take me long.' She couldn't look at him.

'Not tonight.'

There was a sharp note in his voice that drew her gaze, and she saw his face was serious and troubled.

'All right, you make the pudding,' she said.

She was determined to stick to the mundane, Rico realised. That way she could pretend it had never happened. He stared at her, wishing she would tell him everything, knowing that would never happen. 'OK. I did promise to cook for you tonight.'

He could feel the relief radiating from her, but the easy atmosphere they'd shared earlier had gone; they both knew it. He had opened an old wound, and he shuddered to think what that wound might be.

Rico occupied Zoë's mind throughout most of that night. She couldn't sleep and she couldn't think about anything apart from him. She had gone cold and he had gone—no surprises there. His bright golden fritters dressed with fresh lemon juice and vanilla sugar had been a surprise. They'd been truly unforgettable—as had his swift departure the moment he had bolted them down!

He hadn't been able to get away fast enough. She couldn't blame him. They had shared one lovely evening, thanks to Maria. And now, with The Kiss out of the way, at least he knew she wasn't interested in that sort of thing.

She had laid her cards out in front of him. She couldn't be like other women—women who took their right to enjoy physical love for granted. Women like the flamenco dancer on the poster. It was better Rico knew that.

Her ex had been right. She was frigid. And it wasn't that she didn't try—she felt sexy, and she hoped she looked at least a little bit appealing, but as soon as things turned hot she went cold. That was what had happened tonight. No one could change what she was—not even Rico. Thumping her pillows into submission, Zoë settled down to sleep.

Zoë's hands flew to her face. The stinging slap had jolted her whole frame. She could never beg; that was her problem. She could never ask for forgiveness, for understanding, when she didn't know what she had done wrong.

She backed away, stumbling in the darkness, feeling for the furniture to guide her. Finally there was nowhere else to go. She was pressed back against the cold, hard door. She could only stand now, and wait for her punishment. There was no escape. The door was locked. She knew that too, without trying the handle. She knew it just as surely as she knew what was coming next.

She looked at him then, but his face was shadowed and she couldn't be sure who it was. She searched her mind desperately, trying to think of something that would make him change his mind, make him listen to her. But he was already taking off his belt.

This was always the worst part—the waiting. She could hear herself whimpering as she held up her hands to shield her face…

'Oh!' Zoë lurched up into a sitting position, reeling with shock. It took her a few minutes to get her bearings and realise she was safe in her bed at the castle.

Steadying her breathing, she looked around. Of course there was nothing unpleasant in the room. It was quite empty. The castle was completely still. She had heard several doors slamming when the film crew came back from their evening at the café, but it was the middle of the night now; everyone was sound asleep.

Glancing at her wristwatch on the bedside table, she saw that it was three o'clock in the morning. Slipping out of bed, she pulled back one side of the heavy curtains and gazed out to where the castle walls were tipped with silver in the moonlight. Where was Rico now? Where was he sleeping? Was he alone? He had never told her where he lived, and she had never asked. Did he live with anyone? Was he married?

A bolt of shame cut through her. She would never hurt anyone as she had been hurt—yet she knew none of the answers to these questions. She had let Rico kiss her without knowing anything about him, and then she had gone on to betray her innermost fears to him.

Zoë pulled away from the window. Unwelcome details of the nightmare were slithering back through the unguarded passages in her mind. She couldn't shut them out. She had tried that before, but they always, always came back. Rico didn't know anything about her, about her past. How would she bear the shame when he found out? His rejection tonight would be nothing compared to the scorn and contempt he would feel for her then.

In her mind's eye Zoë could already see his face; it was cold and unforgiving. But even that was better than revisiting the dark side of her memories. She could only be grateful that by filling her mind with Rico Cortes she had finally found a way to blot the worst of them out.

Was this how it was always going to be—her ex-husband haunting her for ever?

Yes—if she allowed him to, Zoë realised.

Opening the window as far as she could, she leaned out, drinking in the healing beauty of the mountains.

The moonlight was like a blessing on her face. Closing her eyes, she inhaled deeply. There was a faint scent of blossom on the air.

CHAPTER FIVE

ZOË was up shortly after dawn on Monday. She was skilled at putting the dark shadows behind her, and, though she was tired after her disturbed night, her mind was full of the party the following day. She was determined to have everything ready in good time.

The local producers took a well-earned rest over the weekend, and Monday was the only day the market opened late. That played into her hands, giving her a chance to draw up a schedule and get organised before she went shopping for ingredients. She enjoyed supervising everything—even down to which flowers she would have on the tables.

Taking a glass of freshly squeezed orange juice with her onto the veranda, she perched on a seat overlooking the cypress grove to make her list. It was still cool, and she had taken the precaution of wearing a cosy sweater over her pyjamas. Her hair was still sleep-tangled round her shoulders and for a while she just sat idly, soaking up the view. The air was quite still, apart from the occasional flurry of early-morning breeze, and there were few sounds to disturb her tranquil state other than the birds chorusing their approval of another bright new day.

Closing her eyes, Zoë relished the touch of the sun on her freshly washed face. She breathed deeply and smiled as she inhaled the same scent she had enjoyed the previous night. The cicadas were just kicking off with a rumba. The perfume of the blossom was overlaid with the warm, spicy aroma of Spain. She couldn't have been anywhere else. She didn't want to be anywhere else. Feeling a sudden rush of joy, she stretched out her arms towards the sun—then another sound intruded.

Opening her eyes, she straightened up and looked around, and saw a horse and rider coming towards her at speed. Shading her eyes against the low, slanting rays of the sun, she could just make out the shape of a man crouched low over the neck of his horse. He was galloping flat out towards her, down the tree-lined grove, using the mile-long stretch like his own private racecourse.

'Rico?' Zoë murmured, getting to her feet. Her heart was pounding, and for a moment she panicked. Only an emergency could have brought him to the castle at such a pace.

But then he slowed abruptly, when he was still some yards from the entrance to the courtyard.

Almost as if he knew he was close to water, the horse pricked up his ears and pranced towards the trough located right beneath the veranda where Zoë was standing. The sound of his hooves on the cobbles made her smile. Did everyone dance to the rhythm of flamenco in Cazulas?

The black stallion and his rider were a magnificent sight. Rico was so much a part of his mount it was difficult to tell who made the decisions, and Zoë smiled again in admiration as she raised her hand in greeting. She could ride—but not like that.

Reining in beneath the veranda, Rico smiled up at her.

Zoë was surprised he looked pleased to see her. Had he forgotten what had happened between them the previous night? She had made a fool of herself. So why was he here? What had he come for?

'Buenos días, señorita!' Rico bowed low over the withers of his horse. 'I trust I find you well this morning?'

His uncomplicated greeting bolstered Zoë's determination not to slip back into her old ways. He wasn't being scornful or cruel, he was just saying good morning.

'*Buenos días, señor.*' Planting her hands on the veranda rail, she smiled down at him.

'You look tired,' Rico observed as he sprang down to the ground. Swinging the reins over the horse's head, he tethered him to a pole.

'Do I?' Zoë put a hand to her cheek. She had no intention of telling him why. 'I haven't had a chance to put my make-up on. That must be it.' Then she remembered her shabby old pyjama bottoms, flapping in the breeze beneath her rumpled sweater.

'You don't need make-up.' He took the steps two, three at a time. 'But you do look tired.' Pulling off his soft calfskin riding gloves, he slapped them together in the palm of one hand. 'That juice looks good.'

'It is. I'm sorry, would you like one?'

'Thank you, that would be nice.'

The jug of juice was in the refrigerator in the kitchen. And he would need a glass. She would have the chance to slip out and change into a respectable outfit. 'Please, sit down. I'll go and get the juice for you.'

'I'll come with you.'

'No, that's—' Pointless arguing with him, Zoë thought wryly, leading the way inside.

Every tiny hair rose on the back of her neck at knowing Rico was behind her, and as he held the door for her she could picture his muscles flexing beneath the close-fitting riding breeches, the turn of his calf beneath the long leather riding boots. And that was before she considered the wide spread of his shoulders, the powerful forearms shaded with dark hair, the inky black waves caressing high-chiselled cheekbones, slightly flushed beneath his tan after the exertions of his ride.

She could picture everything about him—his mouth, his lips—she could feel the scrape of his bristle on her cheeks, and she could remember all too clearly that she had pushed him away when he had wanted to kiss her.

Because she was frigid.

It was no use, Zoë realised as they walked into the kitchen. She would never be able to relax with a man like Rico. She would never know what it felt like to be properly kissed by him. But that didn't stop her wanting to.

'The work for this meal isn't proving too much for you?' He looked around when she had given him a glass of fresh juice. 'You seem to have made enough for an army already.'

'I'm never happier then when I'm cooking.' She stared at him as he went to wash out his empty glass at the sink. She was so used to clearing up after people she knew she would never get used to this.

When he had finished, Rico turned back to her. He slipped one thumb into his belt-loop, and before she knew what she was doing Zoë had followed the movement. Feeling her face flame red, she redirected her gaze into his eyes.

'It all smells wonderful.' Rico smiled.

'Thank you.' Zoë's throat seemed to have closed up. The riding breeches moulded him precisely, revealingly—terrifyingly. 'Why are you here?' Her voice sounded faint, and she was glad there was a table between them.

'It's such a beautiful morning I thought you might like to ride out with me—if you're not too busy...'

She could hardly pretend to be when she had been lazing on the veranda when he arrived. 'I've thought about riding lots of times since I got here, but—'

'But?'

'Well, I can't ride like you.'

'There are plenty of quieter mounts than mine to choose from in the stables.'

'I'd really like that.' Zoë frowned. 'But I'd have to change.'

'Go right ahead. I'll wait for you.'

'All right, then.'

Closing the door behind her, Zoë leaned against it for a moment to catch her breath. What was she doing? She closed her eyes. She couldn't let her old life get in the way. She had fought her way out; she wasn't going to slip back now. There was nothing wrong in riding with Rico. She could do with the exercise. The rest of the day was for shopping and cooking, so an hour's recreation would be perfect. In fact, it was just what she needed.

Zoë changed her clothes quickly, putting on jeans and a shirt. When she returned to the kitchen Rico was gazing around at the changes she had made.

'I trust you approve?' Zoë hoped she didn't sound too defensive. He put the pottery dish he had been examining back on the shelf. The changes were small, but it made the place feel like home—and that was no easy task in a castle.

She spent so much time in the kitchen it had to feel right. It was where she prepared everything, painstakingly testing each dish any number of different ways long before the cameras rolled on set. So she had hung some new blinds at the windows to control the flow of light while she worked, and there was a row of fresh herbs lined up in terracotta pots along the window-sill. She loved the local pottery. It was precious in a world where everything was growing more and more alike.

'Wouldn't it have been easier to do the filming in here?'

'Yes, but my director felt there was more space in the hall, so I gave in to him on that point.'

'Your director? He works for you?'

'For my production company.'

'I'm impressed.'

'No need to be. It's not unknown in the television world for people to take the independent route.'

'So whose fault was the set dressing?'

'Mine,' Zoë said quickly. 'I own the company. The buck stops here.'

Rico's lips pressed together as he stared at her, then curved as if he was amused. 'Are you ready to go?' He glanced towards the door.

As he held it open for her, and she walked past him, Zoë felt a tingle race down the length of her spine. The heady scent of saddle soap and leather laced with warm, clean man was overwhelmingly attractive, and her thoughts turned wilfully to what was beneath Rico's breeches. She had never indulged in erotic thoughts before, always dreading where they might lead. But there was something about Rico Cortes that made it impossible to think about anything else.

Daydreaming was a dangerous game…

Once they were outside in the fresh air Zoë knew that at least for the next hour or so she was going to put every negative thought from the past out of her mind.

They stood on the veranda side by side for a few moments, enjoying the view. They were standing very close, close enough to brush against each other, but then Rico's stallion scented his master's presence and squealed with impatience.

'I think he's trying to tell us that he's been kept waiting long enough,' Zoë said.

'We had better go down,' Rico agreed, 'before he pulls that post out of the ground.'

She followed him down the steps.

'We should find you a horse.' Rico tipped his chin towards the stables. 'Before Rondeno breaks free.'

'Rondeno?'

'A native of Ronda. My stallion is named after the most famous of all the White Towns in Andalucia. Ronda is surrounded by rugged mountains that once sheltered bandits and brigands.'

'How very romantic.' And how perfectly suited to Rico, Zoë thought, looking up at him. He would have made a very good pirate, with his swarthy, dangerous looks. Had Rico's career taken a similar path to her own, she could see him as a leading man, breaking hearts on the small screen as well as the large. There was always a hunger for new talent. 'Have you ever thought of acting as a career?'

'Never.' He slanted her a look. 'I prefer reality to fantasy every time.'

'Flamenco, cooking, riding...' She smiled. 'Is there no end to your talent?'

'You haven't even begun to scratch the surface yet.' He laughed. 'Come on, let's get you that horse.'

At a gentle canter, and with the warm wind lifting her hair, Zoë began to wonder if she had ever felt so carefree before. The countryside was bathed in a soft, golden light, and the sky was as clear a blue as she had ever seen.

In this part of Spain the ground was well fed by a fast-flowing river, but now it was approaching the hottest months of the year the water was little more than a sluggish trickle. The pastures in the shadow of the mountains, however, were still green, and provided the perfect ground for riding over.

'We'll stop over there by the bridge.' Rico had brought his stallion alongside her horse, and was keeping pace at an easy canter. 'There should just be enough water for the horses to drink.'

As she cantered ahead of him, Zoë couldn't believe she hadn't ridden one of the horses stabled at the castle before. She had assumed they were in livery for any number of local riders, and therefore not included in her lease. Not so, Rico had explained. They all belonged to the same person—someone he knew, presumably. He knew the horses, and had chosen a quiet gelding for her to ride, saying Punto was perfect for her.

And he was, Zoë thought, patting the horse's dappled neck. Punto was just the type of horse she liked: he was kind, and willing, and wore an American-style high saddle, which was a lot more comfortable than the English saddle she was used to.

Rico's stallion moved ahead as he scented water. Urging her own horse forward, Zoë caught him up by the slow-moving stream. She allowed the reins to fall loosely on Punto's neck and gazed around. Apart from the gurgle of water and the sound of the two horses drinking there was utter silence. Lifting her face to the sun, Zoë closed her eyes, allowing the light to bathe her in its warmth.

'It's so beautiful here.'

'I agree,' she heard Rico murmur.

She longed for him to lean over in his saddle then, and kiss her as he had kissed her before. This time she wouldn't pull back. No bad feelings could intrude here, on such a beautiful day.

But Rico didn't kiss her. He didn't even try to touch her. He just sat patiently, waiting for their horses to finish drinking.

Of course he wouldn't kiss her. Men couldn't stand women who pulled away at the last minute. It was every man's idea of a turn-off. *There were only so many knocks to his pride a real man could take.* Wasn't that what her ex-husband had told her? He was right, and this was the proof.

She collected up the reins. 'I'd better get back to the castle. There's still so much to do. I have to get to the market before all the best produce is sold.' She turned Punto away from the water.

'You don't have to do that,' Rico insisted. 'Why don't I get someone to collect what you need?'

The breeze flipped Zoë's hair from her face as she turned to him. 'That's very kind of you, Rico, but I prefer to choose everything myself.'

'Force of habit?'

'That's right.'

They began to trot, and then the horses broke into a canter.

'So, are you still coming tomorrow?' She had to yell to make him hear.

'Try and keep me away. Shall we race back to the castle?'

The challenge excited her. Urging Punto on, Zoë loved feeling the wind in her hair and hearing the sound of Rondeno's hooves pounding after her. She knew Rico had to be holding back, and, snatching a glance over her shoulder, she laughed with exhilaration. Rondeno was far more powerful than her own mount, but she could almost believe Punto was enjoying this as much as she was.

The control Rico exercised over his mighty stallion was the biggest turn-on of all, and Zoë's heart was thundering louder than the combined sound of both horses' hooves. The friction of the saddle as she brushed back and forth was something new to her. She had never taken notice of it before, but now she was intensely and electrifyingly aroused. Leaning low over Punto's neck, she begged the horse to speed up and carry her away from Rico—and away from temptation.

He had to dig his heels into Rondeno's side to catch up with her. His laugh of pleasure and surprise was carried away on the wind because they were moving so fast. She was quite a woman. He liked her spirit. In fact he liked Zoë Chapman—a lot, Rico realised, easing up so they were galloping alongside each other.

Her lips were parted to drag in air, and there was a faint line of pink along the top of her cheekbones that had not been put there by the wind. Her lips were moist where she had licked them, and when she flashed him a glance he saw that her exquisite eyes had darkened to the point where only a faint rim of turquoise remained.

She was not leading him on even a little bit—she was sexually unawakened. The realisation sent arousal streaking through him like a bolt of lightning. So much sexuality packed into one woman with everything to learn about the art of love. Even if he'd cared nothing for her, he would still have had to find that a turn-on. But after Zoë's fearful response to him sorting her out in the sex department was starting to feel more like a crusade. Her frustration was obvious—something had to give. And he wanted to be around when that happened.

As they approached the castle they both reined in, but Zoë kept the lead. She laughed, and smiled across at him in triumph.

The change in her was striking. Where was the cool professional businesswoman now? Where was the frightened girl who had pushed him away? Right now she radiated confidence. The grey cloud that sometimes hung over her had vanished; he hoped it stayed that way.

She wanted to feel this good for ever, Zoë thought as she sprang down from the saddle. 'Thank you.' She turned to Rico, smiling. 'That was the best time I've had for—'

'Ever?' he suggested.

'I should definitely try to ride more frequently. Perhaps I will, now I know I can take one of the horses from the stables here.'

'The groom will always pick one out for you, or just tell him you prefer to ride Punto.'

'I will.' Zoë rested her cheek against Punto's neck for a moment. 'He's the best—aren't you, Punto?'

'Don't ride unaccompanied until you know the lie of the land better.'

Zoë's pulse began to race as she gazed up at Rico. 'I won't.' It was such an easy promise to make. With Rico riding next to her she would be in the saddle every spare moment that came her way.

'The groom will ride with you if you ask him.'

Somehow she kept the smile fixed to her face. 'That would be great.'

'*Adios*, Zoë!'

'*Adios*, Rico.' He was too busy holding his black stallion

in check to note her sudden lack of enthusiasm, Zoë saw thankfully. 'I appreciate you taking me out.'

'Don't mention it.' He wheeled Rondeno away.

I wouldn't dream of mentioning it, Zoë thought, smiling to herself as Rico cantered away.

Turning, she viewed the elderly bow-legged groom with wry amusement. Riding was definitely crossed off her 'must-do' list for now.

CHAPTER SIX

TUESDAY was almost too busy for Zoë to give much thought to anything apart from cooking—cooking and Rico. Now she knew for sure he was coming, everything had gained an extra impetus. She wanted to make Maria feel she was part of something special, something that gave the exceptional flamenco dancer the recognition Zoë believed she deserved.

She was in the kitchen by nine, having been up at dawn to go to market to find the freshest ingredients for those dishes that could not be made in advance. On her return she had laid everything out on the counter to make one last check. But, however many times she looked at them, she couldn't get past the feeling that there was still something missing.

She had decided upon a menu of clams *à la marinara*, in a sauce of garlic, paprika and *fino* sherry, with an alternative of *zoque*, the popular gazpacho soup made with red peppers and tomatoes. But for the main course she had called upon her secret weapon—a wise old man from the village who seemed to be everyone's *tio*, or uncle. Zoë had been debating over the best recipe for *paella*, and the *tio* was the only person who could advise her properly, according to Maria, who had unexpectedly appeared at her side at the market.

Thanks to the introduction from Maria, the elderly expert uncle had approved Zoë's choice of ingredients, after turning them over and sniffing for freshness. He had even demanded a heavy discount from the stallholders, reminding them, as Zoë would never have dreamed of doing, that they would be eating the food they had just sold to her when they came to the castle for the party that night.

'Locals care more about the rice than the rest of the meal,' the *tio* had said, patting his nose with one finger just as Zoë had seen Maria do. 'It must be well washed if you want the grains to separate, and then the rice must be cooked in fish stock—never water—water is for soup. You must have *caldo*—sorry, broth—for your rice. And the yellow colour of *paella* comes as much from the *noras*—you would call them peppers—as it does from the strands of saffron you add to the broth. Did you enjoy your ride?'

Cooking methods and Rico in the same breath! Zoë knew her astonishment must have shown on her face.

'It's a very small village,' the *tio* had explained with a smile, tapping his nose once again.

So it was, Zoë had thought, as she thanked him for his kindness.

Armed with quite a lot more local knowledge than she had bargained for, she had returned to the castle to prepare the main dish.

Balancing a cheap pan the size of a bicycle wheel on the counter, Zoë laid out pieces of chicken and squid, clams, scampi and *rojas*—large red prawns—with all the precision of a stained-glass window on top of a bed of rice, onion, garlic and peppers. Finally she added three types of beans and then some seasoning. Now the dish was almost ready for the oven.

She paused, inhaling the faint salty tang of the sea rising from the cool, fresh ingredients, her mind straying back to the earlier events of the day. How had the *tio* known she had been riding with Rico? Did everyone in the village know? Was it coincidence that Maria had found her at the market?

Suddenly Zoë wasn't sure of anything. Had she imagined she could ride out with Rico, bathe in his glamour, and get away with it? Frowning, she turned back to her cooking. She had already made some rich fish stock laced with strands of deep red saffron, and she poured that over the raw ingredients. Standing back, she had to admit she was delighted with the finished product.

The *tio's* last piece of advice had been to wrap the *paella* in newspaper once it was cooked. Then the finished dish should be left for ten minutes for the rice grains to separate. But wouldn't the newsprint spoil the striking colours?

Newsprint. Banner headlines. Zoë actually flinched as she turned away.

The icy fingers of the past were with her again, clutching at her heart. *Star Sells Sex.* Three words that damned her for ever in her own mind, even though they were lies. As far as the world at large was concerned, the story had brought her to wider public notice, and, in the topsy-turvy way of celebrity, had actually boosted her career. Going along with public perception had actually helped her to get through things. Keeping a smile fixed to her face had become such a habit that gradually the reality that lay behind the headline had been consigned to the back of her mind like a sleeping monster.

The Zoë Chapman who didn't appear on the television screen or at book signings was careful never to wake that monster—but she knew it would stir if she allowed herself to feel anything too deeply again. The shame, the failure, the brutality that lay behind it—all of that would rise up and slap her down into the gutter, where her ex-husband thought she belonged. So far she had frustrated his attempts to see her eat dirt, but it had been a long road back.

But she *had* made it back, Zoë reminded herself, and that was all that mattered. Every time the past intruded she pictured herself as a cork being held down in the water—she *always* broke free; she *always* bobbed up again. It was only men with brutally strong characters she had a problem with now. Men like Rico Cortes.

She had to get over this—get over him. She had to force her thoughts back on track. Perhaps she would wrap the *paella* in one of her huge, freshly laundered cloths when she removed it from the heat, and allow it to settle that way...

* * *

She could relax at last. The *paella* looked great on camera. It had been filmed at each stage of its preparation, and she had been sorry for the film crew, who had had to carry the loaded pan back and forth between the set in the Great Hall and the kitchen, where she was working.

Philip, her director, was demanding, but he was the best— which was why she had hired him. She trusted his judgement, and his decision to do things this way had kept everyone out from under her feet. Her own 'to camera' shots would be added later, when make-up and wardrobe had been let loose on her. It wasn't easy to cook and appear as cool as a cucumber at the same time.

Now she had finished the *paella*, Zoë's thoughts turned to pudding, which was her favourite part of any meal. She planned to serve a chocolate and almond ice cream, garnished with her own *guirlache*, which was crushed and toasted almonds coated with a sugar and lemon juice toffee. And there would be hot orange puffs dusted with sugar, as well as *figuritas de marzapan*, marzipan shaped into mice and rabbits for the children.

She concentrated hard, loving every moment of the preparation. Cooking was an oasis in her life that offered periods of calm as essential as they were soothing. She counted herself fortunate that her love of food had brought her success.

Resisting the temptation to sample one of everything she had made, Zoë finally stood back, sighing with contentment. It all looked absolutely delicious.

Someone else thought so too—before she knew what she was doing Zoë had automatically slapped Rico's hand away as he reached for a marzipan rabbit.

'Rico!' She clutched her chest with surprise. 'I thought it was one of the crew! I didn't realise it was you…' And then all she could think was that her chef's jacket was stained and her face had to be tomato red from the heat in the kitchen. 'I didn't expect you until tonight.'

'It is tonight.' He gazed past her through the open window. 'I must have got carried away. What time is it?'

'Don't worry. Not time to panic yet.'

Not time to panic? So why was her heart thundering off the chart? Zoë tried to wipe her face on her sleeve without Rico noticing. 'What brings you here so early?'

'I thought you might need some help. It looks like I was right.'

'I'm doing fine.'

'I brought drinks.'

'Drinks… *Drinks!* That was what was missing!' She turned to him. 'I've made some lemonade to pour over crushed ice for the children, and for anyone who doesn't drink…'

'That's fine, but you should have plenty of choice. It's going to be a long night.' Going to the kitchen door, he held it open and a line of men filed in. They were loaded down with crates of beer, boxes of wine and spirits, and soft drinks.

'*Cava*, brandy, sherry, and the local liquor…' Rico ticked them off, shooting an amused glance at Zoë as a man bearing a huge earthenware flagon marched in.

'Oh, no—not that!'

'You don't have to drink it,' he pointed out, smiling when he saw her expression.

'You're far too generous. Of course my company will pay for everything—'

'We'll worry about that later.'

'The crew will drink everything in sight, given half a chance.'

'Not tonight. Just worry about getting the white wine and *cava* chilled.'

'What do you mean, not tonight? Once they've filmed Maria, and taken a couple of crowd shots, the crew will join in the party—'

'Haven't I told you not to worry?' Rico slipped the lead man some banknotes to share around as tips.

'You don't know the crew like I do. I don't want to spoil it for them, but, bluntly, with all this drink around—I just can't face the mess in the morning.'

'Let me assure you that your crew are going to be far too busy to get into any mischief. You have my word on it.'

'Rico, what are you talking about?'

'Your director has arranged for another feature to be filmed tonight. Hasn't he told you yet?'

'No...' Zoë frowned. How could that happen when they always discussed everything in advance?

'He is very enthusiastic.'

'That's why I hired him.' She resigned herself. It had to be something good. She couldn't imagine the man who was the mainstay of her team asking everyone to work late unless it was really worthwhile...

'He's got everyone's agreement to work overtime,' Rico added.

'Can you read my mind?'

'From time to time.'

Zoë looked at Rico, looked at his lips, then dragged her gaze away. 'It must be an excellent feature.'

'Last minute.'

'Yes, I guessed that.' She couldn't be angry with Philip, though she was curious. She welcomed suggestions from anyone in the team. The strength of her company was that they worked together, with no one person riding roughshod over another. She knew from bitter experience that those tactics never worked. 'Do you know what it is?'

'A typical sport of this region.'

'A sport?' Zoë looked doubtful.

'Something colourful and authentic for your programme.'

'Don't tease me, Rico. Tell me what it is.'

'I'm going to get some extra glasses out of the Jeep.' Before Zoë could question him further he added, 'And by the way, *señorita*, your *figuritas* are delicious.'

So what was this surprise feature? Zoë flashed a glance at the door. Rico should have told her. He made her mad, and he made her melt too—a dangerous combination, and not something she should be looking for in a man. She wasn't looking for a man, Zoë reminded herself firmly.

'Tell me about this sport,' she insisted, the moment Rico came back.

Putting the case of glasses down on the counter, he turned to look at her. Zoë tried not to notice the figure-hugging black trousers and close-fitting black shirt moulding his impressive torso, or the fact that there was something wild and untamed about him. It lay just beneath the sleek packaging, telling her he would never settle down. Men like Rico Cortes never did.

'Wrestling.'

'Wrestling!' And then it all fell into place: El Paladín!

She shuddered inwardly. 'Will you be taking part?'

'Perhaps.' He shrugged. 'I've arranged for people to come and wash these glasses for you, and to serve tonight, so that after you finish filming you can have fun too. My people will clear up after the crew. You don't have a thing to worry about. You should kick back a little, enjoy yourself for a change.'

'Thank you,' Zoë murmured, her good manners functioning on automatic pilot. Her brain was working on two levels: the first accepted the fact that she needed help on the practical side because she had promised the crew they could join the party after work; the second level was dragging her down to a place she didn't want to go. Anything that smacked of violence, even a sport, made her feel queasy.

'Wrestling is hugely popular in this part of Spain. When your director asked me about it, I knew I could help him.'

'El Paladín?' Zoë's voice came out like a whisper, and she tried very hard not to sound accusing. It *would* make a good feature. If the programme was to reflect the area properly, it was just the type of thing she would normally want to include.

'I'm always looking for authentic items to bring the programmes to life…'

'It doesn't get more authentic than this.' Rico smiled at her on his way out of the door. 'See you later, Zoë.'

Zoë watched with mixed feelings as the raised square wrestling ring was erected in the middle of the courtyard. A beautiful day had mellowed into a balmy evening, and there was scarcely the suggestion of a breeze. Wrapping her arms around her waist she knew she had to pull herself together and stop fretting. Half-naked men would definitely be a bonus for her viewers. She could do this. She had to do this. How hard could it be?

The ring was almost finished, and people were starting to arrive. Soon it would be showtime. Surely it couldn't be that bad? She wouldn't have to watch it all—though she would have to be in shot for at least some of the time.

Firming her jaw, Zoë took a final look through the ropes at the empty ring. She still had to take a shower and prepare for the programme. Turning back to the castle, she hurried inside.

By the time she returned to the courtyard it was packed. Men had come from all over the region to test their strength. She guessed it was something of a marriage market too, judging by the flirtatious glances several groups of girls were giving their favourites.

The thought of Rico stripping off and stepping half naked into the ring was enough to make anyone shiver. Zoë tried hard not to react when she spotted him at the opposite side of the courtyard, surrounded by a group of supporters. At first she thought he was just greeting friends and she relaxed, but then he stepped away from the others and she saw he was naked from the waist up. Maria and the wise old *tio* from the village were standing with him; it seemed every soul in

Cazulas had come to support him. They were a good-natured group, and cheered him on as he strode to the ringside.

Zoë turned away, but then she guessed Rico must have vaulted over the top rope, because the applause around her was suddenly deafening. She looked up. She couldn't help herself. She had to see him for herself.

He was everything she found attractive in a man—and everything that terrified her too. It was impossible to believe that any of the other men had a physique to equal Rico's, or could match the fierce, determined look in his eyes. He was, after all, the champion. Rico Cortes was El Paladín.

Zoë fought down the panic struggling to take control of her mind. He was about to become a guest on her programme— no one said she had to sleep with him. She shivered, feeling fear and excitement in equal measure as she watched him flex his muscles in the ring. The woman standing next to her shouted something in Spanish, and then grabbed hold of her arm in her enthusiasm.

All the women wanted Rico, Zoë saw when she glanced around. For one crazy moment she felt like climbing into the ring and laying claim to him herself. And then the television lights flared on and she was working.

Smiling for the viewers, Zoë looked properly for the first time at the ring. She had to observe everything carefully so she could provide an appropriate voiceover for the film.

Clinging to her responsibilities certainly helped her through. But how to describe how she really felt at the sight of Rico's smooth, bronzed torso without turning her cookery programme into something for late-night viewing?

His belly was hard and flat, and banded across with muscle, whilst the spread of his shoulders seemed immense from where she was standing. And she couldn't stop her gaze tracking down to where his sinfully revealing wrestling shorts proved that it wasn't just the spread of his shoulders that was huge.

She wanted to look anywhere but at the ring—but how could she when she knew the camera would constantly switch between her and El Paladín? She had to stare up at Rico Cortes, and she had to applaud enthusiastically along with the rest of the crowd.

As the evening wore on the temperature began to rise. Rico was red-hot.

She would see it through because she had to. It was only a sport, after all, Zoë told herself. But by the time the bell rang and the first bout was over she was shaking convulsively from head to foot.

Making her excuses over the microphone to Philip, she eased her way through the crowd and went back into the castle, where she hurried up the stairs to her bedroom. Sinking onto the chair in front of the dressing-table, she buried her face in her hands.

How could she go back? Lifting her head, Zoë stared at her reflection in the mirror. She was pallid beneath her tan, and her hands were still shaking. She tried to apply some fresh lipgloss, and gave up. She couldn't risk a smudge of red across her face. And why was she trying to make herself look appealing? Did she want to attract trouble? Was she *asking for it* again, as she had done in the past?

When the shuddering grew worse, Zoë sat with her head bowed until she'd managed to bring herself back under control. She had to go back outside again eventually. She couldn't let everyone down—not Maria, not the *tio* who had helped her so generously, nor the film crew. And, most of all, she couldn't let herself down. She had fought hard to get her life back. She had to get over this.

There was a soft knock on the door. Marnie, the girl in charge of Wardrobe, had brought her a fresh top to change into. It was identical to the one she was wearing—low-cut and sexy—and the brash cerise looked good with her jeans. It was meant to stand out on camera when she was in a crowd.

It certainly did that, Zoë thought as she viewed herself critically in the mirror. The colour was identical to the skintight flamenco dress the girl named Beba wore on the poster at the mountain hut.

'I'm going to change.' She started tugging off the top.

'You can't, Zoë. What about continuity?'

'I don't care. I'm going to put on a shirt. If we have to reshoot, so be it.' Zoë saw Marnie's expression, but nothing was going to change her mind.

'Do you need me for anything else?'

'Marnie, I'm really sorry. This isn't your fault. Just tell Philip I insisted.'

'Well, it's your programme,' Marnie pointed out.

'Before you go, could you redo my lips?'

'Sure.' Marnie smiled at her.

Marnie applied the lipgloss expertly, with a steady hand. Zoë knew it was more than she could have done. She checked in the mirror. 'That's great. Thank you. I'm sorry to have dragged you up here just for that.'

'As long as I'm back in time to see Rico Cortes in action—' Marnie winked at her '—I'll forgive you.'

Zoë felt a chill strike through her composure, but forced a laugh as Marnie left the room.

She looked fine for the camera. The ice-blue of the shirt looked good against her tan, and complemented her red-blonde hair. She looked far more businesslike. She didn't look sexy at all. It was much, much better.

The shots on set inside the castle went smoothly—too smoothly, Zoë thought, cursing her professionalism. They didn't need a single retake.

'The change of clothes is fine for in here,' Philip advised her. 'But of course you'll change back into that cerise top again for ringside?'

'No, Philip.' Zoë shook her head. 'I'm keeping this shirt on. We'll just say the second half of the competition took place on another day—I don't care, I'm not changing.' She could tell by his face that Philip was taken aback. It wasn't like her to be difficult or unprofessional.

The competition was in its final stages by the time Zoë returned to the courtyard. The noise, if anything, had grown louder. Philip had to cut a path for her through the crowd. Then she realised that he meant her to stand right up at the front, as close to ringside as possible.

'Is this my punishment for changing clothes without warning you?' Zoë had to grab Philip's arm and yell in his ear above the roar of the crowd. She even managed a wry smile. But the moment he left her to return to his cameras Zoë's throat dried.

Philip's voice came through on Zoë's earpiece, testing the sound levels.

'You OK, Zoë? You sound as if you're getting a cold.'

'No, I'm fine—absolutely fine.'

'Then it must be the excitement at seeing all those muscles up close. You can't kid me,' he insisted, 'I know you love it—just like all the other women.'

That was the point. She wasn't like all the other women. *She wasn't normal.*

It was surprising how well you could know people, and yet know nothing about their private lives, Zoë thought, remembering that Philip had once worked for her ex-husband. He had been surprised when she had called time on their marriage, having thought them the perfect couple.

'Do you want me in shot for the presentation of the prizes?' she said into her microphone, clinging to her professionalism like a life raft.

'I'll want a reaction shot. You should have chosen something more glamorous to wear than that shirt. You look so plain!'

Perfect, Zoë thought.

'Never mind. It's too late to do anything about it now. I'll stick to head shots.'

She felt guilty because Philip sounded so grumpy, but it couldn't be helped. She was more concerned about getting through the next few minutes.

Women on either side of her were clutching each other in excitement as they stared into the ring. One of them turned to her, gesturing excitedly, and Zoë looked up. Rico was standing centre stage.

The television lights drained everything of colour, but Rico's torso still gleamed like polished bronze. The ghosts were hovering at Zoë's shoulder as she stared at him. But he was laughing good-naturedly with one of his defeated opponents, and then, leaning over the ropes, he reached out to help the elderly *tio* of Cazulas into the ring.

Zoë frowned. She hadn't expected that. Drawing on other times, other trials of strength, she had expected a grim face, a hard mouth and cruel eyes. But those trials of strength had been no contest. How could there be a physical contest between a woman and a powerful bully of a man?

Watching her elderly friend take Rico's hand and raise it high in a victory salute, Zoë tried to piece together what the *tio* was saying with her very basic knowledge of Spanish. Finally she gave up, and asked the woman standing next to her if she could translate.

'Our *tio* is announcing the prize,' the woman explained, barely able to waste a second of her awestruck gaze on Zoë.

A heavy leather purse changed hands between Rico and the *tio*. 'What's that?' Zoë shouted as cheers rose all around them.

'A purse of gold,' the woman shouted back to her.

But now Rico was passing it back to the *tio*. 'What is he doing?' Zoë said, looking at her neighbour again.

'It is the same every year,' the woman explained, shouting above the uproar. 'El Señor Cortes always returns the purse of gold to the village.'

'And what are they saying now?' Zoë persisted, but the excitement had reached such a fever pitch she couldn't hear the woman's reply. After several failed attempts her neighbour just shrugged, and smiled to show her it was hopeless.

Rico was staring at her, Zoë saw, going hot and cold. What did he want?

Holding her gaze, he walked quickly across the floor of the ring, leaned over the ropes, and held out his hand to her.

Zoë glanced around. No one could tell her what was happening because everyone was cheering and shouting at the top of their voices.

Rico held up his hands and silence fell. Everyone was staring at *her* now, Zoë realised. She couldn't understand it, but then Rico leaned over the ropes again and her face broke into a smile. She reached out to shake his hand, to congratulate him on his win. The next thing she knew she was standing beside him, with the spotlights glaring down on them both, and the *tio* was beaming at her while the crowd cheered wildly.

Rico's mouth tugged in a grin and he held up his hands again to call for silence. After he had spoken a few words in Spanish the cheering started up again. 'I choose you,' he said, staring down at Zoë.

'Me?' Zoë touched her chest in amazement. 'What for?' Her heart was racing out of control. She couldn't think what he meant. She couldn't think—

'You will find out.' Humour warmed his voice.

Zoë laughed anxiously as she stared up at him. She could still feel the touch of his hands around her waist— Her thoughts stalled right there. She might have weighed no more than a dried leaf in his arms. Shading her eyes, she tried to read his expression, but he drew her hand down again and enclosed it in his own.

Taking her into the centre of the ring, he presented her ceremoniously to the *tio*, and Zoë forced herself to relax.

What could happen with the *tio* standing there? She found a smile. These pictures would be flashed around the world. The last thing she wanted was to cause offence to an elder of Cazulas—a man who was her friend.

The *tio* seemed delighted that Rico had 'chosen' her, and embraced her warmly.

'What's all this about, Rico?' Zoë asked the moment the *tio* released her and turned away to address the crowd. Someone handed Rico a black silk robe and she waited while he put it on.

'You're part of my prize,' he said, when he had belted it.

'I'm *what*?'

Before Rico could answer, the *tio* turned around. Television cameras were angled to capture every nuance in Zoë's expression, and she cared for the *tio's* feelings, so she forced a smile.

'Do you understand our tradition?' he said to her warmly.

'I'm not sure.' She didn't want to look to Rico for answers.

'Allow me to explain.' The *tio* made a gesture to the crowd, begging their indulgence. Then, taking Zoë's hand, he led her out of the spotlight.

'It is our tradition. Having won the competition, Rico may choose any woman he wants. He chooses you.'

Incredible! Antiquated! Totally unacceptable! But the *tio* was looking at her so warmly, so openly, and he made it sound so very simple.

'Don't I have any say in the matter?' Zoë was careful to keep her voice light.

'Don't worry—the custom is not open to the same interpretation it might have been fifty years ago, when I was a young man.'

Zoë managed a laugh. 'I'm pleased to hear it.' She smiled at him, and then glanced at Rico. The expression in his eyes suggested he would have preferred sticking to the old ways.

Waves of panic and bewilderment started threatening to engulf her.

'It is a great honour to be chosen,' the *tio* coaxed. 'Look how disappointed you've made the other women.'

Zoë gazed around to please him, but whichever way she turned she saw Rico.

'All you have to do,' the *tio* explained persuasively, 'is to spend one night with him.'

'What?'

'I mean one *evening* with him,' he corrected hastily. 'My English is…' He waved his hands in the air with frustration, making Zoë feel worse than ever.

'I'll do it for you—of course I'll do it. Please don't worry.' This wasn't about her own feelings any more, or just work. It was about showing loyalty to an old man who was only trying to uphold the traditions of his youth. 'I won't let you down.'

Zoë allowed the *tio* to lead her back into the centre of the ring. She wouldn't let him down, but she was damned if she was going to play some antiquated mating game with Rico Cortes. She smiled tensely while the official announcement was made.

'Don't worry, I'll take a shower before I come back for you,' Rico murmured, the moment the applause around them subsided.

'Let's get one thing straight, Rico,' Zoë said, turning to face him. 'I'm grateful you took me riding, and helped me out here with staff for tonight. But I don't like surprises—especially not surprises that affect my work. The television lights are off now, the *tio* has gone to join his friends, and as far as I'm concerned the show's over.'

'And?' His eyes had gone cold.

'And I have no intention of becoming another of your trophies!'

'*Bravo*, Ms Chapman,' he murmured sardonically.

'Why don't you go and take that shower now? There are plenty of bathrooms in the castle.'

Rico's expression hardened as he looked down at her—and who could blame him? Zoë hadn't meant to sound so harsh, but there was an engine blazing away inside her, and a voice in her head that said, *Drive him away.*

What had happened tonight—all the fighting, the sounds, the tension, Rico overpowering everyone… It was just too close to her nightmares. She tried telling herself that all his strength was directed into sport. She had seen him ride; now she had seen him fight. But another side of her said: This is Rico Cortes, El Paladín, the man who conquers everyone with his strength… Her mind was fogged with fear. Unreasonable fear, maybe, but she couldn't shake it off.

The only thing she could latch on to in a world that was slipping away beneath her feet was the thought that she must not let the *tio* down. She would keep her promise to him, spend the rest of the evening with Rico. But first she had to go and seek some space, some cool, quiet place where she could get her head together.

She should fix somewhere to meet up with Rico before she did that. 'When you come back, Rico, I'll be—'

'I'll find you,' he said coldly, swinging a towel around his neck.

He vaulted over the top rope, dropped to the ground, and strode away from her without a backward glance.

CHAPTER SEVEN

THE meal was everything Zoë hoped it would be. The *tio* stood up and told everyone that the *paella* was the best he had ever tasted.

Rico was sitting next to her at the top table. He turned when she sat down after accepting the enthusiastic applause. 'Congratulations, Zoë. This has been a huge success for you.'

He was polite, but then, since he'd decided to trust her he was always polite. She wanted more. 'It's all thanks to the *tio* of Cazulas—' But Rico had already turned away to continue his conversation with the young Spanish beauty seated on his other side.

Zoë's smile faded. Rico had been cool ever since they'd sat down. It was understandable after her behaviour in the ring. But she couldn't tell him why she'd felt so bad after the wrestling. The *tio* of Cazulas had embroiled her in some ancient fertility rite that had fallen flat on its face.

She had kept her part of the bargain, staying with Rico throughout the evening, though he preferred the company of the vivacious young woman sitting next to him. His back had been half turned to her for most of the time.

Zoë noticed people were still smiling at her and raising their glasses. She smiled back, raising her own glass, but it was a hollow victory. She was thrilled everyone had enjoyed themselves, but the one person whose enthusiasm really mattered to her was otherwise occupied. She had thought of changing tables, but it would only cause comment—and Maria would be dancing soon.

There were about twenty people seated around each of the long tables set at the edges of the courtyard. The tables were laden with food, as well as countless bottles of beer, still water, and jugs of wine. She had used red and white gingham tablecloths to add a splash of colour, and placed lofty arrangements of brilliantly coloured exotic flowers on every one. Strings of lights swung gently in the night breeze overhead, twinkling like tiny stars, and waves of conversation and laughter were flowing all around her.

Resting her chin on her hand, she saw Maria's guitarist place his stool in a corner of the performance area. Sitting down, he began to strum some popular tunes. It was all perfect. She had asked to sit at the end of the table so that she could get up easily to supervise the food when necessary. Her plan had worked well—brilliantly, in fact. Though she might as well have stayed in the kitchen. Why hadn't Rico chosen the ebony-haired beauty as his trophy in the first place?

Zoë was distracted from her thoughts by Maria's entrance, and sat up. Straight away it was incredible. The air was charged with energy the moment she appeared. Framed in the doorway of the castle, Maria stood with one hand pointing towards the stars, calling up whatever mysterious energy fuelled her performance. Even Rico had turned to watch, forgetting, at least for a moment, the young beauty at his side.

The guitarist picked out an arpeggio, filling each note with incredible weight and passion. Maria stood unmoving until the last vibration from the strings of the guitar had faded away, and then she stepped proudly into the full glare of the television lights. Hovering like an eagle for an instant, she suddenly moved forward with all the grace of a much younger woman, crossing the courtyard with swift, precise steps.

She came into the centre of the performance area, raised her chin, and stared at some far distant point only she could see. The expression on her face was one of defiance, great pride, and anger, but there was pain and compassion too. Sweeping her crimson skirt off the floor in one hand, she made a powerful gesture with the other, and at the same time struck the floor one sharp blow with her foot.

Philip was by Zoë's side minutes after Maria had finished her performance. 'This programme will go down in history. That woman is superb—they're saying she's even better than Beba—though she's old enough to be Beba's mother.'

'I'm sure you're right.' Zoë frowned, tuning out for a moment. She had never heard of this Beba before in her life, and now she was haunted by the woman.

Philip dashed away before she could ask him anything, and then Maria had another surprise for them. She came back into the centre of the courtyard and invited everyone to join her in a dance.

Strictly speaking, this was country dancing, the *tio* said when he came over to explain what was happening to Zoë. All Zoë knew was that Rico's seat, as well as the one next to him, was empty, and what he and his young partner were doing on the dance floor was more dirty dancing than country dancing.

'Rico is good, eh?' the *tio* said, following her interest keenly. 'But the girl is too obvious. No subtlety.'

No subtlety at all, Zoë agreed silently. The young woman was like a clinging vine, all suckers and creeping fingers.

'Why don't you dance?'

Zoë turned to smile at the *tio*. 'With you?' She started to get to her feet.

'No, not with me!' The *tio* pressed her down in the seat again. 'I mean you should dance with Rico.'

'Rico is already dancing with someone,' Zoë pointed out, trying her best to sound faintly amused and casually dismissive.

'Here, in this part of Spain,' the *tio* told her slyly, 'women do not wait to be asked.'

Zoë turned to stare at him, wondering if she'd heard correctly, but instead of explaining himself the mischievous old man drew his shoulders in a wry shrug.

There were a million reasons why she could not—should not—do as the *tio* suggested, Zoë thought as she stood up. This was insane, she told herself as she walked towards the dance floor. Rico Cortes would simply stare at her and turn away. As for his young partner—Zoë could just imagine the look of triumph on her face when Rico told her to get lost. She was about to make a fool of herself in front of the whole village—the whole world, if you took the television cameras into account. But she just went on threading her way through the crowds on the dance floor.

'*Brava, Zoë! Eso es!*'

'Maria!'

'You should have worn your performance dress,' the older woman whispered in her ear before melting back into the crowd.

Too late for that now—jeans and a tailored shirt would have to do. She couldn't stop to think about it, Zoë realised as she reached her goal. She tapped the young Spanish beauty lightly on the shoulder. 'Excuse me. I'm cutting in.'

'*Qué?*'

The girl couldn't have looked more shocked. Zoë almost felt sorry for her. Almost. She didn't have a chance to see the expression on Rico's face; the next thing she knew she was in his arms.

'Well, this is a surprise.'

She could feel his breath warm against her hair. 'A pleasant one, I hope?'

'Unexpected, certainly.'

He had changed into casual clothes for the party: blue jeans, shirt with the sleeves rolled up and the collar open at the neck. He smelt divine, and he felt...

Zoë shivered as the music slowed to a sensuous rumba rhythm, as if responding to her mood. She saw that the young girl had quickly moved away to dance with some people of her own age, and didn't seem too upset—though right at this moment Zoë had decided to be selfish. She only cared how *she* felt. And she felt wonderful.

Having so many people around them gave Zoë the confidence to relax in Rico's arms. As they brushed past people smiled with approval. Whether that was to show their appreciation of the party or because she was in Rico's arms, Zoë didn't know, and right now it didn't matter. Even with the difference in their size they fitted together perfectly. They were dancing as one, as if they had always danced like this, and the planes and curves of his body invited her to mould against him.

Rico had an innate sense of rhythm, and Zoë could only be grateful that Maria had given her the courage to dance in a way that made her feel seductive and desirable. Nothing existed in her universe outside of Rico as they danced on to the haunting music, and Zoë barely noticed when one of his powerful thighs slipped between her legs, bringing her closer still. She only knew that it felt right, essential to the dance, and now they were one—moving as one, breathing as one, and dancing as one...

He let her go when the melody turned to something lively. Zoë realised that they had been the centre of attention, and that now couples were turning to their own pleasures again. It was true, she had been so deeply and sensually aware of Rico she had forgotten for the space of their dance that they were not alone.

She trembled as Rico stared down at her. The tempo of the music had increased, but they were both oblivious to it. Nothing existed outside the ambit of his gaze, and as she watched his lips tug up in a smile Zoë realised she was hoping for something more.

'Shall we?' He tipped his chin in the direction of their empty places at the table.

She dropped back into the real world. Of course Rico didn't want to dance with her all night. People were staring. The music had stopped again, and she was still standing on the dance floor like a fool.

'I'll...go and see if there's any pudding left. Someone might be hungry.'

Rico didn't try to stop her as she struggled to make her way through the whirling couples, but then she realised he was beside her, shielding her with his arm. When he stopped to talk to an old acquaintance she slipped away, making for the door to the kitchen. But she hadn't even had a chance to close it when Rico came in behind her.

'What's wrong with you, Zoë? Why are you running away from me?' He leaned back against the door, and she got the impression he wasn't going anywhere until she explained.

'Nothing.'

'Nothing?' His voice was flat, disbelieving. 'I think it's time you told me what all this is about, don't you? You were fine when we were out riding together, and then tonight you turn on the ice.'

'You haven't spoken to me all night!'

'Do you blame me?'

Truthfully, she didn't.

'Then you come up to me and want to dance. And then you run away again.' Rico made a sound of exasperation as he spread his arms wide. 'Are you going to tell me what all this is about?'

'I can't—'

'You can't?' He shook his head. 'Why not, Zoë? You've never been short of opinions in the past.'

'I can't explain because you'll just think I'm being ridiculous.'

'Try me.'

She met his gaze, and this time neither of them looked away.

'Violence frightens me.' Her voice was just a whisper.

'Violence?' Rico frowned and straightened up.

'Of any kind. I know how that must sound to you—and I do know wrestling's just a sport—'

'Are you saying I'm a violent man?' His eyes narrowed, and she could see she had offended him deeply.

'No—not you...' Zoë's voice dried. She looked away.

'Are you saying I remind you of someone who was violent in your past?' He looked stricken. 'That's it—isn't it, Zoë?'

'I can't help it.' She made a weak gesture with her hands.

'Do you have any idea how insulting that is?'

She saw his hand tighten on the door handle until his knuckles turned white, and took a step towards him. 'I'm sorry, Rico. I haven't even congratulated you—'

He made an angry gesture, cutting her off. 'I don't know what shocks me the most—the fact that you can mention violence in your past as if it were nothing, or the thought that you could possibly confuse me with some snivelling bully who preys on women and others who are weaker than himself.'

'I just don't want tonight to be all about me. This is your night too, Rico.'

'What you've just said overrides anything else.'

'We can't talk about it now. I can't just abandon my guests.'

'Forget the damned party!'

'How can I?' Zoë said, moving towards the door. 'It's wrong of me to keep you so long like this, Rico. Your young companion—'

'Will do perfectly well without me.' He caught hold of her arm as she tried to move past him. 'You can't leave it like this, Zoë. If you are protecting someone—someone who's hurt you—'

'I'm not,' she said steadily, meeting his eyes. 'I promise you, Rico, it's all over now.'

'Is it?'

'Yes,' she said, holding his gaze. 'Yes, it is.'

He shook his head, and his eyes were full of concern. 'Know this, Zoë: I am not and never have been a violent man. I have never raised my hand in anger to anyone. When you have great strength the very first thing you must learn is control. Strength has not been given to me to use against a weaker person, or some helpless creature. It has been given to me to help other people when I can, and for me to enjoy. Nothing more.'

And before she could say another word, he added in a fierce undertone, 'And don't you ever confuse me with some other man again.'

Rico opened the door for her and stood aside to let her pass, and the happy noise and bustle of the courtyard claimed her.

'*Señorita?*'

Zoë looked round to see that he had followed her out. It took her a moment of recovery after their highly charged exchange for her to realise what he meant to do.

Sweeping her a formal half-bow, he offered her his arm. 'May I escort you back to the party, Señorita Chapman?'

The rest of the night passed in a blur of laughter and dancing for Zoë. By the time people started drifting away her feet were aching. She had joined in every traditional dance of the region—men, women and children, all on their feet, colourful skirts flying and proud hands clapping the irresistible syncopated rhythms.

Now she was exhausted, and more grateful than ever to Rico's efficient staff, who had cleared away absolutely everything from the hall, leaving her with nothing to do there.

'Why are you back in the kitchen?'

'Rico—you caught me.' Zoë turned, embarrassed that he had seen her stealing her own *figuritas*. Now it was her turn to get her hand slapped—the only difference was, Rico's slap was more of a caress, and then he raised her hand to his lips. 'You have earned a break, Zoë.' He looked around. 'My people are only too happy to clear up—I told them they could take anything that was left home with them.'

'Oh, I'm sorry.'

'Don't be. I'm sure they can spare you one marzipan mouse.'

'Why are you frowning?'

'I just don't have the knack of dismissing the things you told me—as you seem to have.'

'Have I spoiled the party for you?'

'Don't trivialise what you said, Zoë. You can't keep everything locked inside you for ever.'

Why not? She'd been doing a pretty good job up to now. 'Let's not talk about it tonight,' she said, forcing a bright note into her voice. 'We're both tired—'

'Are we?'

Heat flared up from Zoë's toes to scorch her cheeks. 'Is it a deal? Can we just leave all the other stuff for another time?'

Pressing his lips together, he frowned. He didn't look keen. 'If that's what you want. I don't want to spoil the night for you.'

'You could never do that.'

The suggestion of a smile tugged at his lips.

They broke eye contact at a knock on the door. She couldn't have given a better cue herself, Zoë realised as Rico's helpers trooped in. It was impossible to talk about the past now. 'Shall we go back to the party?'

'Not for too long.'

There was something in the way he said it that made Zoë blush. 'Why?' She looked up at him, and immediately wished she hadn't.

Dipping his head close as he opened the door for her, he

whispered in her ear: 'I'm tired of playing games, Zoë. Can't you see how much I want you?'

It was so unexpected. She couldn't imagine anyone other than Rico even saying the words. No man had ever admitted to wanting her—he was the first. She didn't know how to answer him. She didn't know what was expected of her. 'I don't want to talk about—'

'Who said anything about talking? And you have my word I won't make you do anything you don't want to do.'

Rico drew her out of the bustling kitchen through a door that led into the silent hall. 'That's better,' he murmured, pulling her close to drop a kiss on her brow. 'I like to see you smile. I don't want to see you tense and unhappy ever again.' Nudging her hair aside, he planted a second tender kiss on the very sensitive place below her ear.

When he rasped the stubble on his chin against her neck Zoë gasped, and allowed him to draw her closer still. It was so easy to slip beneath Rico's seductive spell. She could have broken away at any time; but his hold on her was so light there was no reason to try.

She parted her lips, welcoming the invasion of his tongue, but he teased her gently, pulling away until she locked her hands behind his neck and brought him back again. And then their mouths collided hungrily, and it was Rico's turn to groan as she moulded into him.

She was in a dream state as Rico led her swiftly by the hand through the castle. Every part of her was aching for his touch. His hand was firm and warm, and she went with him willingly through the archway that led to the luxury spa.

'I haven't been down here before,' Zoë admitted as Rico let go of her for a moment to close the door. She couldn't bear the loss, and reached for him.

'Not yet,' he warned, his fingertips caressing her cheek.

'Why not?'

'Because it's better this way.'

She followed him down a short flight of marble steps.

'Are you sure you have never been down here before?' Rico stopped at the bottom and turned to look at her.

'Never.'

'Then you're about to get a very pleasant surprise.'

Zoë watched Rico punch a series of numbers onto a panel on the wall. A door slid behind them. 'What are you doing?'

'I've changed the code so we won't be disturbed. Zoë?' Rico touched her face with one fingertip when he saw the expression on her face. 'The code is twenty-one, twelve—my birthday. Don't look so worried. You can leave any time you want.'

'I just thought if there was an emergency—and I needed to get out in a hurry—'

'An emergency?' Rico smiled. 'What? You mean something like this?'

And then somehow she was in his arms again, and he was kissing her so tenderly, so thoroughly, Zoë wondered how she remained standing. Heat flooded through her veins, and when his tongue tangled with her own a soft moan came from somewhere deep in her chest, showing him how much she wanted him to kiss her.

When he pulled back, she reached up, wrapping her arms around his neck to mesh her fingers through his hair and draw him close again. When Rico kissed her she felt no fear. She wanted him to know how she felt, that she was ready for him: moist, swollen, hot. But then she remembered…

'First ice, and now fire?' Rico murmured, looking down at her.

He was so tender, so caring—but how could she be sure he wouldn't be shocked or disappointed when she experienced the painful spasm that had always made fully penetrative sex impossible for her? She had to be sure she wouldn't stop, Zoë thought as her hand strayed to his belt buckle…

Rico moved her hand away, bringing her fingers to his lips

to kiss each tip in turn. Zoë's eyes filled with hot tears of failure.

'You need to slow down, Zoë.'

Glancing up uncertainly, she saw his lips were curving in a smile. She started to try and say something, to explain herself, but, putting one firm finger over her lips, Rico stopped her.

'I'm going to find you something to wear in the hot tub.' He broke away. 'And then I'll order some refreshments for us from the kitchen.'

Something to wear? Food from the kitchen? She was so naïve! She had expected to be naked, feeding on him.

'And then we'll sample the hot tub together.'

Better.

She gazed around. The ancient walls had been sandblasted in this part of the castle until they were pale yellow. The floor was a mellow golden marble, and all the tiles and fittings had been selected with a view to nothing startling to the eye or the senses. The temperature was perfect, the silence complete.

Rico reached inside a beautiful old oak chest and brought out some fluffy caramel-coloured towels, then black swimming trunks for himself and a swimming costume the same shade as her eyes.

'That's a lucky find.'

'Or good planning,' Rico said.

'You know your way around here pretty well.'

'I should. The castle belongs to a very good friend of mine. Do you want to go and change now? Music?' he added, handing her the costume.

'Why not? Something gentle and soothing would be nice.'

'I'll see if I can accommodate you.' His voice was ironic as he moved to select a CD.

A sinuous melody started weaving its spell around Zoë as Rico took hold of her hand again, and she went with him, deeper into the spa.

The hot tub in the centre of the floor was illuminated by hundreds of flickering candles. Zoë gasped. 'How—?'

'You ask too many questions. Just accept you're going to be pampered for a change.'

There were a million questions she would have liked to ask him, but for once in her life she bit them back.

They changed in beech-lined changing cabins, and she covered her costume with one of the white towelling robes hanging on the back of each door.

'To think I didn't even realise this place existed!'

'The hot tub is kept locked up for most of the time.'

'Your friend must like you a lot to let you use it.'

Loosening the belt on his robe, Rico let it drop to the floor. Zoë kept her gaze strictly confined to his face, but to her relief saw the black bathing trunks in her peripheral vision.

'Aren't you going to take your robe off?'

'Yes…yes, of course I am.'

Zoë waited until she was up the steps of the hot tub and had one leg in the water before slipping off the robe. Then she was in like a flash, submerged beneath the water before Rico had even climbed in.

There were tiny lights above her head, winking on and off in a deep blue ceiling decorated with puffs of smoky cloud to give it the appearance of a night sky. 'This is unbelievable.' Zoë sighed, stretching out her arms along the top of the tub to keep her balance in the swirling water. She leaned her head back, and closed her eyes.

'I prefer an open-air bathroom.'

She looked up again. Rico had settled himself across from her. 'You mean the sea?'

A door opened before he could reply to her, and a waiter came in with a tray of refreshments for them.

'Thank you,' Rico said, glancing round at the man. 'You can leave them here.'

Zoë blinked. There was champagne on ice, two tall crystal

flutes, a bowl of sweet wild strawberries, some whipped cream and a bowl of chocolate sauce on the tray. 'Now I have seen everything.' She shook her head incredulously.

'You really think so?'

Rico's voice was challenging, and soft. She didn't answer.

Wrapped in fluffy towels, and stretched out on a recliner next to Rico's, Zoë sipped champagne while Rico lay back watching her through half-closed eyes.

'If this is the Cazulas way of thanking people for giving a party, I may have to stay a lot longer than I planned.' Putting her glass down, she relaxed back against the soft bank of cushions and stretched out her limbs in languorous appreciation.

Selecting a plump strawberry, Rico dipped it in rich chocolate sauce. 'Open your mouth.'

He touched it to her lips, and she could smell the warm chocolate sauce. She wasn't quick enough, and it started escaping in runnels down her chin. Leaning over her, Rico licked it off, and then he was kissing her—kissing her deeply.

It was the taste of Zoë that made him greedy. It made him want more, a lot more of her. It made him want everything. But he knew better than that. He knew he had to wait. Pulling back, Rico saw that her eyes were still closed, her lips still slightly parted as she sucked in breath, and there were smudges of chocolate all round her mouth.

'Don't be mean,' she whispered, opening her mouth wider. 'I want more.'

Smiling wryly, Rico began to feed her again. He kept on until she was begging him for mercy as she laughed; until she couldn't keep up with the chocolate sauce and the cream, and it dripped onto her breasts, and slipped between them. Her lips were stained red with strawberry juice and her eyes were almost as dark as the chocolate. And then he couldn't help himself. He was kissing her again, and she was clinging to him, not caring that her towel had fallen away.

Zoë gasped as Rico's tongue began to lave between her breasts. She had sunk lower and lower onto the recliner, wanting him to continue until every scrap of chocolate had disappeared. Her breasts were streaked with juice and cream, and there was a coating of chocolate on each painfully extended nipple. His tongue was deliciously warm, and rasped against her sensitive skin in a way that was unbearably good.

She wanted more. But Rico was heavily into foreplay—something she had never experienced before. He knew how to tease and torment her; he knew every erogenous zone on her body. Her flesh sang with pleasure as she writhed beneath him, and she could no longer make any pretence at shyness. How could she, with his warm breath invading her ears? She cried out to him, shuddering uncontrollably, but just as she did so he pulled back.

Short of grabbing him by the hair and forcing him to suckle her breasts, she had no idea what to do next. She was getting desperate. 'Shall I feed you now?'

Holding himself up on his fists, Rico looked down at her. 'What did you have in mind?'

There was such a wicked smile tugging at his lips, Zoë couldn't resist it. 'Just this.' Cupping her breasts, she held them out to him.

CHAPTER EIGHT

RICO stared at Zoë's breasts. They were magnificent—a fact he had been trying hard to ignore from the moment he had seen her in a tight top pulling plastic oranges down from the walls. His control had never undergone such a painful test—especially now, when she was warm, soft, and more lovely than ever. But was she ready for this?

He couldn't stop looking at her tight, extended nipples, currently reaching out to him in the most irresistible invitation.

'Wrong colour?' she teased him softly.

'Perfect.' And they were—the most delectable shade of shell-pink.

'Wrong size for you?'

She was still smiling, waiting, her eyebrows arched in enquiry as she stared at him.

'Zoë—' Rolling off his recliner, he hunkered down by her side. 'What would you like me to do, Señorita Chapman?'

'Eat me.'

'Eat you?' He pretended surprise. 'That's very forward of you...'

'Yes, isn't it?'

Taking matters into her own hands, she sat up and locked her hands around his neck to bring him down to her.

Swearing softly in his own language, he pulled back, drawing her with him, staring into her face as he unlocked her hands. Laying her back down on the narrow couch, he took a long, lazy look down the whole lovely, naked length of her. 'Wild cat!' he murmured approvingly.

There was barely an inch of Zoë's body that had been spared the chocolate, the cream, or the sweet red strawberry juice. He applied himself first to the task of cleaning her breasts, using long greedy strokes of his tongue. With each caress she cried out—he might have been inside her, so intense was her response.

Had she never experienced foreplay in her life? He thought not. When he suckled her nipples she moaned rhythmically in time with his actions until he knew he had to stop. He had never known anything like it before; he had never been so aroused before. His senses were on fire and his anticipation of his final possession of her was overwhelming in its intensity. But before he realised what she meant to do she had surprised him.

Scooping up some sticky chocolate sauce, she smeared a handful over his chest. When she began to lick it off, he knew he was in danger of losing control for the first time in his life. Capturing her in his arms, he rolled with her onto a soft rug on the floor, straddling her, and pinning her arms down above her head. Trying to keep her still while she wriggled beneath him was almost impossible. She was moving her head from side to side, laughing and threatening him in the same breath. Finally securing her wrists in one strong fist, he reached for the cream jug with his free hand, and emptied the contents all over her.

Shrieking with surprise, and laughing at the same time, she tried to break away, but when he started lapping at her belly she changed her mind. Meshing her fingers through his hair, she was all compliance, all sensation, as she told him she wanted more. And when he moved lower, nudging her thighs apart, she whimpered with pleasure and angled herself shamelessly towards him.

He stopped just short of where she wanted him to be, making her cry out with disappointment. Before she had a chance to complain any more, he sprang to his feet and swept her into his arms.

The moment had come, Zoë thought, laying her head on

Rico's shoulder. As he carried her across the relaxation room she knew she trusted him completely. By the time they reached the wet room she was shaking with anticipation. She had never been so aroused. This time Rico would make everything right.

Zoë shrieked as she landed with a splash in the hot tub. Moments later Rico was in with her, holding her safe above the water. Reaching for a sponge, he began soaping her down until all the chocolate and cream had disappeared.

He had never been called upon to exert so much control in his life, Rico realised when they'd got out and he had reclaimed his sanity beneath an icy cold drench shower. And he had never had so much fun with a woman.

Wrapping a towel around his waist, he stared at Zoë drying her lush red-gold hair. She looked more beautiful than ever. Her cheeks were still flushed from their seductive play-fight, and her eyes were gleaming as if her zest for life had suddenly increased. She was starting to trust him, Rico knew, and they could never make love until she did. He only had to touch her, to kiss her, to look at her, to know how inexperienced she was. And it troubled him to think what might have happened to her in the past.

She was humming softly to herself, staring clear-eyed into the mirror as she arranged her hair like a shimmering cape around her shoulders. When he walked up to her, and she looked at him, he could feel his heart pounding so hard in his chest it actually hurt.

It seemed that whatever ghosts there were in her past, or in his, they had no power when they were together. He felt a great swell of happiness inside him. It was a dangerous development, and one that made him feel unusually vulnerable.

Dropping a kiss on Zoë's shoulder, he went to get his clothes. He felt a lot more than lust for her. Her innocence had touched him deeply. Was this love?

When he was almost dressed she came to him. Standing

close behind him, she placed her hands on his shoulders. He felt her rest her face trustingly against his back. And in that moment he knew the whole world and everything in it was his.

He wouldn't have agreed to spending the night in separate rooms at the castle for anyone but Zoë, Rico realised, calling a halt to his pacing. She might be a successful career woman, but beneath the gloss of achievement he knew she was terribly vulnerable, and it made him feel protective, even responsible for her.

It was unusual—no, unique—to find someone so tender and pure. Gold-diggers disgusted him, and there were so many of them around. He had closed his mind years ago to the possibility of ever finding someone who cared for him, and not for his money. Zoë didn't need his money, but even if she had, he knew she would have been as sickened as he at the thought of using a person's wealth as a measure for their worth. It warmed him just to be thinking about her. This was special. She was special.

Going to the open window, he planted his fists on the sill and leaned out. A silver-pink dawn was creeping up the sides of the snow-capped mountains, and the sight bewitched him. Zoë would be sleeping now. He smiled to think of her curled up in bed, sleeping the deep, untroubled sleep of the innocent.

Gazing along the balcony they shared, Rico noticed that her window was open. Her career absorbed her completely. She had to be exhausted.

He turned to look at the computer screen. There was nothing yet.

Natural caution made him investigate everyone who threatened his privacy. He knew already that Zoë was no self-seeking adventuress, but his night-owl investigator had been on the case since she'd arrived in Cazulas. It was a juggernaut he couldn't stop now. He had keyed in his password, and expected an e-mail at any time. Once his mind was set at ease, he would go and wake Zoë in a way he knew she would enjoy.

Just the thought of rousing her from sleep, all warm and tousled, and kissing her into the new day had been enough to keep him from his bed. He was eager to be with her. Throwing back his head, Rico let out a long ragged sigh of frustration. It was hard to believe that here, in one of the remotest regions of Spain, fate had put him on a collision course with someone as honest and forthright as Zoë. He was tempted to go to her right now, without waiting for reassurance.

He tensed abruptly, all senses on full alert. Pushing back from the balcony, he strode quickly to the door. He stood outside his room, in the corridor, and listened intently. He thought he had heard a cry. But there was nothing. He turned, knowing everyone in the castle was asleep. Some nocturnal animal must have disturbed him.

Going back into his temporary study bedroom, Rico closed the heavy door carefully. That was it! He cursed himself for not thinking of it sooner. The doors in the castle were so heavy no sound could possibly penetrate them.

Walking onto the balcony, he quietened his breathing and listened outside Zoë's window. At first there was nothing aside from the soft swish of fabric as the fine voile curtains billowed in the early-morning breeze. Then he heard her cry out again, and, reaching through the window, he turned the key in the double doors and stepped into her room.

She was just awake, and clearly confused.

'Zoë—what is it?' He knelt down at her side. She was as beautiful as he had imagined, still warm from sleep and more lovely than any woman had a right to be if a man was to remain sane.

'Rico.' She pressed her hands against his chest. 'Rico, I'm fine. I'm really sorry if I woke you—'

'You didn't wake me. I'm still dressed,' he pointed out. 'But as for your being fine—I'm sick of that word. You're not fine.'

'All right. I had a nightmare.'

'A nightmare?' He turned away. 'You cried out, and I was worried about you—'

Her face went bright red, as if it was she who was in the wrong.

'You don't need to worry about me.'

He was amazed to see how quickly she could recover her composure. Then he remembered that she was used to covering up the truth.

'As I told you, Rico. There's really nothing to worry about.'

'How long are you going to lie to me about this, Zoë?'

There was a long silence, and then she said, 'I don't know what makes you say that.'

'I heard you this time. I heard you cry out. And then, as I came into your room, I heard what you said.'

She covered her face with her hands, but he couldn't let it rest now. 'Don't,' he said softly. Gently taking hold of her hands, he lifted them away. 'You were in the throes of something much worse than a nightmare, Zoë. You were crying out, begging—'

'No!' She shouted it at him, and he waited until she grew calm again, holding her hands firmly between his own.

'Begging?' She forced out a laugh. 'You're mistaken, Rico—'

'I am not mistaken. And I'd like to know what made you call out—''Please, don't hit me again.'''

'I've told you, you're wrong. I would never say something like that. Why should I?'

'That's what I'm trying to find out.'

She shook her head, and her eyes wore a wounded expression. 'Is that why you were so gentle with me, Rico? Is that why you won't make love to me? Is that why you agreed to stay over in a separate room? You feel sorry for me—'

'Don't be so ridiculous!' He raked his hair in sheer exasperation. 'I don't spend time with women because I feel sorry for them.'

'How many women?'

'Why are you doing this to yourself, Zoë?'

'I tell you, Rico, you're wrong about me.' She scrambled upright with the sheet firmly clutched in her hand. 'You don't need to feel pity for me. It was just a nightmare. Nothing more.' She shook her head, seeing the disbelief in his eyes. 'I'm really grateful you came in to make sure I was all right. You're kind—very kind—and thank you—'

'Don't!' His voice was sharp as he put his hand up. He regretted it immediately, seeing her flinch. 'I would never hurt you.' His voice was just a whisper, but she had already gathered herself into a ball and pulled the sheet up to her chin. 'Don't ever thank me for being kind to you, Zoë. It's the very least one human being can expect from another.' He was consumed with relief when she lifted her head and looked at him.

'Who hurt you, Zoë?'

'No one…'

Her voice was tiny, like a child's, and it hurt him more than anything he had ever heard. 'Is that why you were crying out?' he pressed gently. 'Were you remembering what had happened to you?'

'Rico, please.'

He could feel the anger pumping through him. His hands, balled into fists at his sides, ached with tension. Who could ever hurt her? It was inconceivable to him that anyone could wish to harm one hair on her head. He wanted to protect her—but how could he when she insisted on pushing him away? 'Won't you trust me enough to tell me, Zoë?'

'I can't. I just can't.'

'Please, don't shut me out. I want to help you, but I have to know the truth—'

'The truth?' Zoë made a short incredulous sound. She hated herself as it was for her weakness. How could she know she would cry out when she was sleeping? 'Do *you* always tell the truth, Rico? Do you?'

He couldn't answer her. How could he when he had been staring at a computer screen half the night? They were both victims of the past in their own way. Suspicion was branded on his heart, but Zoë was damaged too, and her wounds had been carved far deeper and more cruelly than his.

Standing up, he moved away from the bed, carrying the image of Zoë in his mind. Her hair was like skeins of silk, gleaming in the moonlight, and her skin was so soft and warm. The room was filled with the scent of the orange blossom she always wore. As he turned, she turned too, and their eyes locked. He longed to tell her everything. He wanted nothing more in all the world than to take her in his arms and keep her safe for ever. But he could not. Instead, he would go back to his own room and maintain his vigil until the information he had asked for came through.

'Goodnight, Zoë.' He walked onto the veranda, closing the doors softly behind him.

Throwing his head back, with his eyes tightly shut, he let out a heavy sigh. For the first time in his life the price he had to pay for being Rico Cortes was far too high.

CHAPTER NINE

CLUTCHING the receiver between neck and shoulder while she scooped up her discarded nightwear from the floor, Zoë listened patiently. There was an opportunity to do a live interview with a national television show—a roving reporter had just arrived with a camera crew. Could she make it in time?

She looked like hell after her disturbed night. She felt like it too, especially remembering what had happened with Rico. But this was work, and there was nothing on her face that make-up couldn't fix. Her heart was another matter, but that would have to wait.

She was curious, and she was tempted too. The publicity would be great for the series—and she was interested to find out why someone from such a well-known show had come all the way to Cazulas to speak to her. Of course the last series had been a big success, and it had generated a lot of media interest. That had to be it.

'Of course I'll do it,' she said, decision made. 'Half an hour suit you? OK, fifteen minutes,' she conceded. 'But get Marnie and the girls up here right away with the war paint.'

Philip had told her there would be a chance for a run-through first, so there would be no surprises and nothing for her to worry about. It was just what she needed to take her mind off Rico... He must have gone by now. There wasn't much to keep him at the castle. But she still had her career. The thrill of the places it took her to, and the amazement that she had made something of herself after all, in spite of her ex's assurances that she never would, had not diminished. She hoped they never would.

She had to stand under a cold shower to try and put Rico

118

out of her mind. Finally, reasonably focused on work and totally frozen, she rubbed herself down vigorously with a towel.

There was a bad feeling niggling away inside her, Zoë realised as she dressed. It made no sense. She had done this sort of thing lots of times before, and knew that nothing was left to chance. It might all appear impromptu at home, but the groundwork had already been covered so that none of the questions came out of the blue. And yet...

'To hell with it,' she murmured, spritzing on some perfume. She was a seasoned campaigner and there was nothing to worry about.

Seasoned campaigner or not, she hadn't factored quite such a bubbly young presenter into the equation. The latest in a long line of glamorous young women with an incisive mind, she was the type of person that Zoë found wearing, but fun in short bursts. They talked through the questions, and decided on the best strategy to adopt to promote the show. Zoë was confident she could keep things moving forward smoothly. They were going to film outside, with a backdrop of mountains behind them, and went on air almost immediately.

'So, Zoë, how does it feel to be here in such a fabulous location, as opposed to being stuck in an overheated studio?' The girl fanned herself extravagantly and smiled, as if this made them comrades in adversity.

Her openness made Zoë laugh. 'It feels great, Lisa—but it's hot outside here, as well as under the lights. Don't forget this is Spain—'

'You've got quite a glow going on there, Zoë.' The girl cut across her, facing the camera to address the viewers. 'Could this be something more than a suntan? I hear the Spanish men around here are quite something. Or *man*, rather,' she added as Zoë stared at her. 'Come on, you can tell us—we won't tell a soul, will we?' she exclaimed, turning again to include several million viewers.

'Let's talk about the programme first.' *And last,* Zoë thought, keeping a smile on her face while her mind raced. They hadn't planned to touch on anything other than her new television series. In fact she had made a point of insisting there would be no delving into her personal life. The past was just that—behind her. That was what she and the young reporter had agreed on.

'You're right, Zoë. Let's talk about your programme. That's what we're here for.'

Zoë stalled. The look on the girl's face was open, inviting... Inviting what? There was just enough guile in her eyes to churn Zoë's stomach. 'I think this series is going to be my best yet—'

'You only *think*? Don't tell me Zoë Chapman's become a shrinking violet?'

'Sorry?'

'You're not going to turn coy on us now, Zoë, are you? Disappoint the viewers?' The girl turned to camera and made a moue, but there was a shrewd gleam in her eyes when she looked back. 'After spending the night as the prize of a wealthy man?'

She had just managed to leave out the word *again,* Zoë thought, feeling the blood drain from her face.

'That's right, isn't it, Zoë?' The girl's lips pressed down as she shrugged and managed to look ingenuous for the camera. 'I've seen the footage.' Her eyes opened really wide and she stared around, as if seeking confirmation that her reportage was absolutely accurate from some unseen source.

Zoë's gaze iced over as she waited for the bombshell to fall. After all, the camera never lied...

'Half-naked men wrestling beneath the stars in this sultry Mediterranean climate—and the champion, El Paladín, also known as Alarico Cortes, claiming you as his prize for the night.' She stretched, showing off her taut young belly as if she had all the time in the world to deliver her *coup de grâce*. 'Mmm, sounds pretty hot to me. *He's* pretty hot!'

'That was just an item.' Zoë tried to laugh it off and put on a good-humoured smile for the camera. Inwardly she was seething. The girl's agenda was obvious. This wasn't about her series. There was still mileage in the old scandal.

'Just an item!' The girl cut her off with a short, incredulous laugh. 'OK, Zoë, let's cut to the chase. You bagged Alarico Cortes for one glorious night. I'm only quoting the age-old tradition here in Cazulas, Zo—no need to look at me like that. Alarico Cortes, if you don't know of him at home, is only *the* most eligible bachelor in Spain—a billionaire, and a good friend of the Spanish royal family. So, what was it like? How does it feel, mingling with the aristocracy? And were you really just a prize for the night? Or is this love?'

Alarico Cortes? Aristocracy? Billionaire? Zoë was stunned. If what the young reporter said was true… The last way she would have wanted to hear it was like this.

'I was lucky enough to be invited to take part in a traditional celebration that has been upheld here in Cazulas for centuries. It was great fun—nothing more than that. I'm really sorry to disappoint you.' She finished with a good-natured shrug towards the camera. Game, set, and match, she thought, seeing the girl's face turn sulky.

'Well, you heard it here first, folks.' The reporter quickly recovered. 'The most beautiful celebrity chef on the circuit has something really special in the pipeline for all of us. Don't miss Zoë's new series, or you'll miss those yummy men— and we're talking drop-dead gorgeous in the case of Alarico Cortes, girls. Thank you, Zoë, for sparing us these few precious minutes away from your show.'

'My pleasure,' Zoë said, with a last cheery smile to the viewers. 'Thank you all for your time.'

She even thanked the girl again when the cameras had stopped rolling. They both knew who had come out on top, and Zoë was determined to remain professional to the last. But she couldn't quite believe she had allowed herself to be set up. It had been two years since the scandal broke. Two years to learn caution. She'd thought she was too wary to be trapped like this—but apparently not.

And Rico Cortes, all round good-guy and local one-man protection agency, had been lying to her all along: his *friend's* castle, his *friend's* horses, the down-homey camaraderie of the flamenco camp—and he was a Spanish grandee. Why wasn't she surprised? It all made sense now. He had been lying to her ever since that first meeting, pulling the wool over her eyes, confusing her with his sweet talk and worthy notions. And wasn't she a chump to have thought him any better than her ex? Rico Cortes was one smart operator.

'Great job, Zoë!'

Zoë looked at Philip blankly as he clapped her on the back.

'Our ratings will soar if you keep this up.'

'That's fantastic.' She was already running towards the castle. She had no idea if Rico would still be there. Inside the castle—*his* castle!

Pausing for a moment in the middle of the courtyard, she looked around. Rico's castle. His village, his horses, his spa, his kitchen, his bed, his office. Shading her eyes, she stared up at the balcony they had shared, and in that moment she hated him.

Zoë walked straight into the study bedroom where Rico had been sleeping. At least now he was gone she could use the computer to let her far-flung family members know the interview would be repeated on breakfast television throughout the morning.

'Rico!' Zoë's heart lurched as she saw him, and her eyes filled with tears as he moved away from the computer screen. 'I thought you would have gone by now.'

'I came back.'

'What are you doing?'

'Don't you knock before you enter a room?'

The situation had an element of farce. He was looking at her with a face full of mistrust and anger when *she* was the one who had been wronged. Rico had been lying to her all along—misleading her, pretending to be a local man when he was... She didn't even know who he was.

'I still hold the lease on the castle. Technically this is my room, Rico.'

Tension stretched between them. Whatever he had on the screen, he didn't want her to see it, Zoë realised. 'I'd like to use the computer now, if you don't mind.'

'There's some data on here I can't afford to lose.'

'So save it. My mails are urgent too.'

'Is something wrong?'

'Plenty. But right now I want to contact my family, because I've just done an interview for TV—' She stopped as he made a contemptuous sound. 'What's wrong with you?'

'An interview?' The look he threw her was full of disdain.

'Yes, an interview, Rico—for my new cookery series. Now, if you don't mind—'

'Nothing else?'

Zoë looked at him. 'What are you getting at? Are you worried I might have talked about you, Rico? Let the world know I bagged myself a really rich man—a billionaire? A real live Spanish grandee and good friend of the King?'

When he said nothing, it was Zoë's turn to make a low, angry sound. 'Have you finished with the computer yet?' she demanded, planting her hands on her hips.

'Help yourself,' he said, moving away from the screen.

She didn't need to read the tall, bold letters on the monitor. They had been branded on her mind two years ago. They were lies. Everyone who knew her, who cared about her, knew that. Facing up to them was the only way she knew to snuff out their power.

Star Sells Sex.

Turning to look at Rico, Zoë could read his mind. He had believed the truth about her, and now he believed the lies. And his pride wouldn't allow him to accept that he had been so wrong about her. He believed she had sold herself for money. The thought turned Zoë cold, drained her of feeling. As Rico thought so little of her, perhaps he had her pegged as a gold-digger, after his money, all the time. Perhaps he had even set up the interview to shame her in public... He couldn't believe he had been so mistaken about someone. Neither could she, Zoë realised sadly.

'Are you expecting a reaction from me, Rico? Heated denials—hysterics, possibly?' She could see he was surprised she was so calm. 'This all happened a long, time ago.'

'Two years ago, to be precise.'

'Well, it feels like a lifetime to me.'

Time flew, Zoë reflected. Two years since her ex-husband had tried to destroy her career. She had been so set on rebuilding her life she had hardly noticed how quickly the time had passed. She could still remember the burn of shame when she'd first read the headline. How could she have known then that the old adage would prove true? There was no such thing as bad publicity; this morning's interview had only proved it yet again.

It was two years since her notoriety in the 'Star Sells Sex' scandal had put her name on everyone's lips. Almost immediately her cookery programme had begun to break every ratings record. Her next step had been to form her own company, and that had led to even greater success.

These days the headline was hardly ever mentioned, and on the few occasions when it was people laughed with her, as if it had all been nothing more than a rather clever publicity stunt. She knew the truth behind the headline, and it couldn't hurt her now. Only Rico could do that, if he believed the lies.

'So you've nothing to say in your defence?' he said. 'No explanation to offer me at all?'

'Am I supposed to ask for your forgiveness?'

'The whole scandal blew over quite quickly.' He shrugged. 'That's why I couldn't place you at first.'

'True.' Zoë smiled sadly at him. 'Did you hope I was hiding something, Rico—so that you and I could be quits?'

A muscle worked in his jaw; other than that there was nothing, until he said, 'Do you blame me for being defensive?'

A short sound of incredulity leapt from Zoë's throat.

'If I had told you who I was from the first moment we met—'

'I wouldn't have thought any more or any less of you.'

They stared at each other in silence for a moment, and then, leaning in front of Zoë, Rico clicked the mouse and cleared the screen.

Straightening up, he gazed at her. 'My full name is Alarico Cortes de Aragon. I have many business interests, but flamenco is my passion, and Castillo Cazulas, as I'm sure you have already worked out, belongs to me.'

'When were you going to tell me, Rico? After we'd slept together?'

'Don't speak like that, Zoë. You must understand I have to protect my position.'

'*Your* position? And I have nothing worth protecting—is that it? I was nothing more than an entertaining diversion while you toured your estates in Cazulas?'

'Zoë.' Rico reached out to her, and then drew back. 'Try to understand what it's like for me. I have to know who I'm dealing with.'

'What are you trying to say, Rico?' Zoë said softly. 'A man as important, as rich and influential as you, has to be cautious about the type of woman he takes to bed?'

'It's a lot more than that, Zoë, and you know it.'

'Do I?' She smiled faintly. 'I'm afraid I must have missed something.'

'Can you imagine my shock when I read this headline?'

'It must have been terrible for you.'

'Don't be sarcastic.'

'How do you expect me to be? You tell me you have to protect yourself from me as if I'm some piece of dirt that might tarnish your lustre.'

'Don't say that. I asked for this information before I knew you, Zoë.'

'And now you do know me,' Zoë said bitterly, glancing at the screen. 'You must be glad that you took that precaution.'

'You don't know me very well.'

'I don't know you at all.'

The coldness in her voice, the bitterness in her eyes cut right through him. He wasn't sure about anything any more, Rico realised. He had spent most of his adult life protecting himself from the gutter press. It was ironic to think that it was their common bond. He focused on her face as she spoke again, and was shocked to see the pain in her eyes when she gazed unwaveringly at him.

'I don't have anything concrete like a headline to shake the foundations of my belief in you,' she said. 'All I have are candles, a romantic night in a beautiful luxury spa, and the horrible suspicion that maybe you arranged all that because you wondered if you had what it took to seduce a frigid woman.'

'How can you say that?'

'You seem shocked, Rico. Why is that? Because I'm getting too close to the truth?'

'No!' The word shot out of him on a gust of loathing that she could even think such a thing. 'It isn't true. I don't know what's happened to you in the past, but you're not frigid. And I don't need the sort of reassurance you seem to think I do!'

'You lied to me.' Her voice was low, and cruelly bitter. 'You made assumptions about me, Rico. You invaded my privacy—that same privacy that's so precious to *you*, El Señor Alarico Cortes de Aragon! *You had me investigated.*' She ground out each word with incredulity, and then gazed up at the sky to give a short, half-sobbing laugh. 'And while that was going on you tried to get me into bed. And then—' She held up her hand, silencing his attempt to protest. 'Then you sold me out to the tabloids for some type of sick revenge.'

'Zoë, please—'

'I haven't finished yet!' She shouted the words at him in a hoarse, agonised voice, leaning forward stiffly to confront him, her face white with fury. 'To cap it all, you turn all self-righteous on me—pretending it matters to you that someone else hurt me, used me as a punch-bag—as if you care any more than he did!'

'You've gone too far!' He couldn't hold back any longer. 'How dare you compare me with that—that—'

'What's the matter, Rico? You think of him and you see yourself? Even you can't bring yourself to admit what you are.'

'And just what am I?'

'A deceitful, lying user!'

'User?' He threw his hands up. 'Who's using who here, Zoë?'

'That's right—stay up in your ivory tower, where you're safe from all the gold-diggers, why don't you, Rico? Only I don't want your money—I never did. I can manage quite well on my own!'

'And that's what you want, is it, Zoë—to be on your own?'

'What do you think?' she said bitterly.

'Then I'd better leave.'

'That would be good.'

'You signed the lease on the castle. You can stay until it runs out. Do whatever the hell you want to do! I'll see myself out.'

CHAPTER TEN

HE'D been thrown out of his own castle. That was a first. Rico looked neither left nor right as he strode purposefully across the courtyard towards his Jeep. Throwing himself into the driver's seat, he slammed the door, breathing like a bull. The knuckles on his hands turned white on the steering-wheel.

They wanted each other like a bushfire wanted fuel to sustain it. They were burning so hot they were burning out—burning each other out in the process. He had seen her muscles bunched up tight across her shoulders. And she wanted to believe him—that was the tragedy of the situation. They wanted each other, they wanted to believe in each other, to be with each other and only each other—but they were tearing each other apart. They needed each other—but she didn't need him enough to tell him the truth. She didn't trust him. Maybe she would never trust him. Could he live with that?

The answer was no, Rico realised as he gunned the engine into life. Some of it he'd worked out for himself—the rest he could find out. But that wasn't what he wanted. He wanted her to tell him. She *had* to tell him if there was anything left between them at all. If she was the victim, not the architect, of that newspaper headline, why the hell didn't she just come out and say so? Maybe there was a grain of truth in it—maybe that was why she couldn't bring herself to explain.

Her accusers were guilty of making a profit out of the scandal—but newspapers were in business to make money, not friends. He had been shocked when he'd read the torrid revelations, but he had to admire her. She was a fighter, like him. But was she fighting to clear her name or to put up a smokescreen? Would he ever know?

Trouble was, he cared—he really cared—and it made him mad to think that all the money in the world couldn't buy him the whole truth. Only Zoë could give him that.

Rico's eyes narrowed and his mouth firmed into a flat, hard line. Thrusting the Jeep into gear, he powered away. She was entitled to stay on at the castle—he had no quarrel with that. He had always rattled round the place. Though it was certainly a lot more lively these days, he reflected cynically, flooring the accelerator pedal.

He eased the neck of his collar with one thumb. He was restless, frustrated—even a little guilty that he hadn't stayed to fight it out with her. He shouldn't have left with so much bitterness flying between them. He should have finished it or sorted it. But how could he when she had made such vicious accusations? The very idea of losing control to the extent that he'd hurt anyone, let alone a woman, revolted him. And then to accuse him of setting up that interview. He made a sound of disbelief. Didn't she know how deep his resentment of trash journalism went?

Rico frowned, gripping the wheel, forcing himself to breathe steadily and wait until he had calmed down. Gradually the truth behind the furious row came to him, as if a mist was slowly lifting before his eyes. He could see that the level of Zoë's passion was connected to the level of pain she had inside her. The legacy of her past had just played out between them. Instead of being hurt and offended by her accusations, he should be relieved that she had finally been able to vent her feelings, and that she had chosen to do it in front of him.

She was right. They both needed space, time to think. When he was with her his mind was clouded with all sorts of things that left no room for reason. He had never felt such a longing for anything or anyone in his life. Just the thought that some-one—some man—some brute—had hurt her made him phys-ically sick. So why wouldn't she let him in? Couldn't she see

that he would take on the world to make things right for her
again? Why wouldn't she trust him?

Swinging onto the main road, Rico channelled his frustration into thoughts of exposing all the bullies in the world to
public ridicule. It would be too easy to use strength against
them; strength of mind was more his speciality, and a far
better tool to drag Zoë back from the edge of the precipice
that led straight back to her past.

As he settled into his driving he suffered another surge of
impatience. It was so hard to be patient where Zoë was concerned. He had to remind himself that she was worth all the
time in the world, and that he hadn't made his fortune by
acting on impulse. And, yes, she was right. He had expected
an emotional response from her when she saw the screen full
of huge letters, each one of them condemning her. He respected that. The headline was more than two years old, but
he couldn't believe she had ever reacted to it in any other
way. It took real courage to handle it so well.

But he had seen her lose control later. Was it his betrayal
that had forced her over the edge even when she could keep
her cool under fire from the tabloid press? If so, did that mean
there was something really worth fighting for growing between them?

Quite suddenly the newspaper article seemed ridiculous.
Zoë had forged a successful career for herself; she had no
need to sell anything other than her talent. But where sex was
concerned she was seriously repressed. He had firsthand experience to back that up...

Remembering, Rico grimaced. He felt like hell. What had
he done? What had he done to Zoë? He should have been
there for her. He should have made allowances. He should
have proved to her, as well as to himself, that he understood
how complex she was. She wasn't like other women, she had
been right about that—but not in the way she thought. Her
past had left her damaged, and instead of trying to help he

had trampled her trust into the ground. There wasn't a brazen bone in her body, and if he had to delve deeper into her past to find out the truth and make things right for her, then he would.

Why was it so important to her that Rico Cortes knew the truth? Zoë wondered as she closed the door on the study bedroom after sending her e-mails. She had been so sure she wouldn't care, so certain she would brazen it out if he looked at her with scorn and contempt. He had done neither, but still the matter wasn't resolved in her head. She had to see him at least once more to sort it out. She had thought she could treat him like anyone else—if he believed the lies, so be it; if he didn't, so much the better. But now she knew she wouldn't rest until he knew the truth.

Her ex had planted the headline—though Rico couldn't know that. He had taken his revenge when she'd left him after years of abuse. She had refused to accept the public humiliation two years ago, and she wasn't about to let it get to her now.

What hurt her far more was the fact that Rico Cortes was a man she might have loved, and that he had deceived her into believing he was nothing more than a local flamenco enthusiast. She could accept his need for caution; Rico was a very rich man indeed—and an aristocrat, according to the search engine on the computer. But he was a self-made man for all that; he had started with nothing but a title.

As she pushed open the kitchen door and walked inside Zoë made a sharp, wounded sound. She was just Zoë Chapman, marital survivor and cook—hardly an appropriate match for a billionaire aristocrat.

She had allowed herself to develop feelings for a man she could never have. Right now she wished she'd never come to Spain, had never met El Señor Alarico Cortes de Aragon, because then he couldn't have broken her heart.

* * *

Arriving back at his beach house, Rico tossed the keys of the Jeep onto the hall table and smiled a greeting at his butler.

'A package arrived for you, sir, while you were out.'

'Thank you, Rodrigo.' Rico scanned the details on the well-stuffed padded bag as he carried it through to his study.

Before opening it he pulled back the window shutters so that brilliant sunlight spilled into the room. His whole vision was filled with the shimmering Mediterranean, and he drew the tang of ozone deep into his lungs. Simple things gave him the greatest pleasure. These were the real rewards of extreme wealth: the rush of waves upon the sand, the seabirds soaring in front of his windows, and the matchless tranquillity.

Opening the package, he tipped the contents onto his desk. There was a log of Zoë's everyday life back in England, along with diaries, tapes, transcripts of interviews, photographs, press-cuttings… Rico's hand hovered over the disarray, and then he pushed it all away.

He didn't want to read what someone else had to say about Zoë. He didn't care to acknowledge the fact that his pride and his suspicion had demanded such an invasion of her privacy. He felt dirty, and disgusted with himself, as if the contents of the package somehow contaminated him.

If he cared to look, he knew that whatever he found in the newspaper cuttings would be a sensationalised account. Even the most respected broadsheet had to succumb to such tactics in a marketplace where fresh news was available at the click of a mouse.

Coffee was served to him, and taken away again without being touched. The crisp green leaves of a delicious-looking salad had wilted by the time he absent-mindedly forked some up.

Pushing the plate away to join the rest of the detritus on his desk, he stood up and stretched. Walking over to the window, he was not surprised to see how low the sun had dipped in the sky. The colours outside the window were spectacular, far richer than before, as if the day wanted to leave behind a strong impression before it gave way to the night.

He would not let Zoë go. He could not. If she told him to go again, then he would still let her stay on at the castle as long as it suited her. It was a hollow, unlovely place without her.

After a quick shower and a change of clothes, he didn't wait for the Jeep to be brought round to the front. Sprinting down the steps, he jogged down the drive towards the garage block and, climbing in, switched on and powered away.

He found her in the kitchen, eating with the crew. They were relaxing in the way only good friends could relax—some with their feet up on the opposite chair, men with their shirts undone, sleeves rolled back, and girls with hardly any make-up, and real tangles rather than carefully tousled hair. The table was littered with the debris of a put-together meal, and when he walked in a silence fell that was so complete it left the walls ringing. There was the sound of chairs scraping the floor as everyone stiffened and straightened up. He could sense them closing in around Zoë like a protective net.

Her lips parted with surprise as she stared at him. She was wearing nightclothes—faded pyjamas—with her hair left in damp disarray around her shoulders. She looked to him as if the day had been too much for her and she couldn't wait to get it over with and go to sleep. Someone at the table must have talked her into joining them for a light meal.

It was the enemy camp, all right. Every gaze except for Zoë's was trained on his face. These were the people who had stood by her, who had stayed with her when she'd made the break from the television company run by her ex-husband. That much he'd learned from the Internet. These were the people who had put their livelihoods on the line for Zoë Chapman.

He waited by the door, and she half stood. But the girl sitting next to her put a hand on Zoë's arm.

'You don't have to go, Zo.'

'No, no… I'll be all right.' She pushed her chair back from the table and looked at him. 'I have to get this sorted out.'

He went outside, and she followed him. 'Will you come with me?' He glanced towards the Jeep.

'I'm not dressed.'

If that was the only reason, he'd solve the problem for her. Striding quickly back into the castle, he plucked a shawl down from a peg. As he came out again he threw it round her shoulders. 'You'll be warm enough now.'

'It's not that, Rico. I'm not sure I want to come with you.'

She took a step away from him. Folding the shawl carefully, she hung it over her arm, as if she wanted time to put her thoughts back in order.

'Please.' He wasn't good at this, Rico realised. He could negotiate his way in or out of anything to do with business. But feelings—needs—they were foreign to him, an emotional bank accessed by other people. He was a man of purpose, not dreams—but quite suddenly he realised that purpose and dreams had become hopelessly intertwined. 'Just give me an hour of your time. Please, Zoë. That's all I ask.'

'Will you wait in the Jeep while I get changed?'

He would have waited at the gateway to hell if she had asked him to.

Rico's knuckles were white with tension by the time Zoë emerged from the castle. She hadn't kept him waiting long, and now he drank her in like a thirsty man at a watering hole in the desert. She was wearing her uniform of choice: jeans and a plain top. She looked great. She was so fresh, so clean, and so lovely, with her red-gold hair caught up high on the top of her head in a band so that the thick fall brushed her shoulders as she walked towards him.

'Are you sure we can't talk here—or in the garden?'

'I'd like to show you something,' he said, opening the passenger door for her.

After a moment's hesitation she climbed in. He felt as if he had just closed the biggest business deal of his life. Only this was better—much, much better.

'What a fabulous place,' she said, when they turned in the gates at the beach house. 'Whose is it?'

Her voice tailed off at the end of the question, and he knew she had already guessed. Sweeping through the towering gates, Rico slowed as they approached the mansion. Even he could see it was stunning now he saw it through Zoë's eyes.

'It's all very beautiful,' Zoë said, when they were inside.

He watched her trail her fingers lightly over the creamy soft furnishings as they walked through the main reception room. Everything looked better to him too now she was here. He could see how well the cream walls looked, with smoky blue highlights provided by cushions and rugs, and the occasional touch of tobacco-brown. The walls had been left plain to show off his modern art collection.

'Chagall?' She turned to him in amazement.

He felt ashamed that he took such things for granted. Not for him the colourful poster prints that had adorned his mother's home and made it so cheerful. He liked the real thing, and he could afford it now—Hockney and Chagall were just two of his favourites. He envied the expression on Zoë's face. He wanted to recapture that feeling. He wanted to remember how it had felt to attend his first fine art auction sale, where he had vowed one day he would be bidding.

Zoë turned back to the picture again. She had never seen anything like it outside a museum. The picture showed a handsome man embracing a woman with long titian hair. They were both suspended in an azure sky, with the head of a good-natured horse sketched into the background. A happy sun shone out of the canvas, turning the land beneath it to gold.

'It's genuine, isn't it? This isn't a print?'

'That's right.' He felt shame again. Such things were meant to be shared. When was the last time he had brought anyone into his home?

'I saw a Chagall in Las Vegas—a man and woman, head to head—' Zoë stopped talking, realising they were standing head to head too, and that Rico was smiling down at her.

'You know what I mean.' She waved her hand and moved away, going to stand by an open window. 'Rico, why am I here?' she said, still with her back turned to him.

'I know everything about you.'

'Oh, do you?' she said, managing to sound as unconcerned as if they had been discussing a new style of drapes.

'Zoë, please, can't we talk about it?'

'Why should we? What purpose would it serve?' She turned round to stare at him.

'Will you come with me?' he said.

Something in his expression made her walk towards him.

This must be his study, Zoë realised. It was a pleasant, airy room, but small on the scale of other rooms in the mansion. It was cosy, even a little cluttered. This was the hub around which the rest of his life revolved, she guessed.

'Please sit down,' he said, holding out a chair for her across from his own at the desk.

'I'd rather stand.'

'Please.'

She didn't want to make a fuss.

'Why didn't you tell me?' Rico said, sitting across from her.

'Tell you what?'

'That all that nonsense in the newspaper was a pack of lies?'

'Because I don't feel the need to defend myself.'

'Nor should you.'

Glancing down at the desk, Zoë realised that all the papers

she had thought were Rico's were, in fact, her own history in print. 'So now you know.'

'I only wish I'd known about it sooner. Why didn't you tell me?'

'Because it's none of your business. And because I don't want, or need, anyone's misplaced sympathy.'

'Misplaced?' Rico sprang to his feet and planted his fists on the desk, leaning so far over it their faces were almost touching. 'A man who is supposed to love you beats you up, and you call my sympathy misplaced? You build a whole new life for yourself, and a successful career, only to have that—that—' Rico stopped, the words jamming in his brain as he searched for something to properly describe what he thought of Zoë's ex-husband.

'I finally left him when he tried to sell me to someone he owed money to.'

All the emotion was gone from her voice. He wanted her to rail against her fate, to show some emotion.

'It was just a night of sex, to pay off the debt...'

'Just! Zoë, Zoë—' Rico passed his hand across his eyes, as if it would help him to make some sense of what she was telling him. Walking around the desk, he drew her to her feet. 'Come with me.' He took her to the open window. 'Look out there. Tell me what you see.'

'It's night-time—'

'It's nature, Zoë—pure, harsh, and lovely. Here at my beach house, and at the castle in Cazulas, I escape from the world when I need to. That's why I was so protective of my privacy when you arrived. Why I still am so protective—but now I want you to have the same. I don't want you to live with a nightmare stuck in the back of your mind. I can't bear to think of you trapped like that, in the past.'

Wrapping her arms around her waist, Zoë inhaled deeply, and then turned away from the window to face him. 'I got away, in case you're interested. I could see the man's heart wasn't in it. False bravado brought him to me after a few drinks with my ex-husband. I just explained it was a bad time for me—that there had to be some mistake. He didn't lose face. There was no unpleasantness. I think I handled it well.'

Handled it well? The words tumbled around Rico's head as if someone was knocking them in with a hammer. He wanted to drag her into his arms right then, tell her it would be all right from now on, that he would be there for her, to protect her from harm. He wanted to promise her that she would never have to face such a monstrous situation in her life again—but she was already walking towards the door.

'Will you take me back to the castle now?'

'I'll do anything you want me to.'

She smiled faintly at him, as if to acknowledge his understanding without necessarily accepting that it helped or changed anything for her.

The call came when Zoë had just climbed into bed, and for the second time that night she rushed to pull on her jeans. This time she tugged a sweater over the top of her tee shirt. She didn't know how long she would be, or what might be involved. She just knew she had to be prepared. A phone call from Maria in hospital was serious. Snatching up her bag and some money, along with her car keys, she hurried downstairs.

Zoë felt as if there was a tight band around her chest until the moment she reached the small private room and saw Maria sitting up in a chair beside the bed with a rug over her knees. 'Thank God you're all right,' she said, crouching down at her side. 'Is it serious?' She reached for Maria's hand. 'I've been so worried about you. Will it affect your dancing?'

Maria lifted her other arm from beneath the blanket, revealing strapping. 'Thankfully just a sprain—nothing more. The X-rays have confirmed it. I'm sorry if I frightened you, Zoë. I just couldn't stand the thought of being here all night, and I have such a thing about taxis—'

'No. You were absolutely right to call me. I'm so relieved. I don't know why, but I thought you might have injured your leg.'

'My fault. I should have explained, instead of just saying I had fallen. I can see now that my legs would be the first thing you thought of.'

'Has anyone told Rico? If he hears you are in hospital he'll be very worried.'

'I tried him first,' Maria told her. 'But he wasn't at home.'

No, he was taking me home, Zoë thought, feeling doubly guilty knowing Maria had probably rung Rico to take her to the hospital. And she had been so lost in her own thoughts on the way back to the castle she hadn't spoken a word to him.

'The main thing is that no permanent harm has been done,' Zoë said, returning to practical matters. 'Can you leave now, or must we wait for a doctor?'

'The doctor has to formally discharge me before he goes off duty for the night. But we can talk until then.' Maria stopped and viewed Zoë with concern. 'You look exhausted, Zoë, is something wrong?'

'No.' Zoë forced a bright note into her voice. 'Nothing.' Nothing apart from the fact that Rico knew the whole sordid truth about her now and she would probably never see him again. He'd been sympathetic enough, but, remembering how he had deceived her about his identity, she couldn't help wondering if his sympathy had just been an act too.

She refocused as Maria started to speak again.

'Are you sure that son of mine hasn't said something to upset you?'

'Your son?'

'Rico?' Maria prompted.

'Rico!'

Zoë turned away. Why hadn't she thought of it? Why hadn't she seen it before? Rico's defensive attitude towards

Maria when she had first wanted to approach her... She had thought it pride on his part that she, a stranger, had dared to expect such an artist to put her talent on show for commercial gain. And the attention he paid Maria, his obvious pride in his mother's cultural heritage. All this should have told her. But how could it be? He was not Rico Cortes, local flamenco enthusiast, but El Señor Alarico Cortes de Aragon, a grandee of Spain.

'I don't understand.' She turned back to Maria.

'It is very simple—'

'You don't have to tell me,' Zoë said quickly. 'It's none of my business.'

'I'm not ashamed of what I did. Rico's father was the local landowner. His wife was dead, and we loved each other. We never married, but I gave him a son.' She smiled.

'But how did Rico inherit the title and the castle?'

'There were no other heirs. His father insisted the title must be passed to Rico. They were very close. It was just the title— his money went to the village.'

'But what about you?'

'I was proud—maybe too proud.'

'But Rico was a success?'

'A huge success,' Maria agreed with a wry laugh. 'Rico has always supported me, and eventually he made enough money to buy back the castle. As his father suspected, Rico didn't need his money—he was quite capable of making his own fortune.'

'You must be very proud of him.'

'I am,' Maria assured her. 'And now Rico cares for the village just as his father used to do.'

Maria's glance darted to the door. She was growing anxious, Zoë realised. 'I'll go and find the doctor, and see if I can hurry him up.' Another thought struck her. 'Did you try Rico on his mobile?'

'Yes,' Maria said, her dark eyes brightening as she looked towards the door.

CHAPTER ELEVEN

HAD Maria planned this? Zoë wondered. She couldn't see how that was possible—unless Rico had said something to his mother, and then Maria had put in a call to both of them, using her misfortune as a mechanism to bring them together.

Her heart was hammering louder than Maria's shoes had ever thundered on a floor as Rico moved past her to draw his mother into his arms. Pulling back, he spoke to her quickly in Spanish. Having received the answer he hoped for, he smiled and kissed her cheek before turning to Zoë.

'Thank you for coming, Zoë.'

How could I not? Zoë wondered. 'I was only too pleased I could help. But now you're here I'll leave you with your mother—'

'No.' Rico touched her arm. 'It's late, Zoë. You should not be driving home alone.'

'I'll go and find the doctor before I leave, and send him in to you.'

'No.' This time he closed the door. 'I'm taking you back with us, and that's final. You've had a shock too, and the roads can be dangerous at night.'

No more dangerous than they had ever been, Zoë thought. But Rico's expression was set, and she didn't want to make a fuss in front of Maria.

They settled Maria into her cosy home in the centre of the village, and then got back in the Jeep.

'It really was good of you to go to the hospital for Maria,' Rico said as they moved off again.

'I'd do anything for her,' Zoë said honestly, resting back against the seat.

'I can see you're tired. I'll take you straight back.'

'Thank you.'

So much for Maria's machinations. If it had been a plan at all, nothing was going to come of it. And of course she was relieved...

Clambering into bed and switching off the light, Zoë sank into the pillows, shot through with exhaustion. It had been quite a day. Her body was wiped out, but her mind refused to shut down. Turning on the light again, she thought about Rico, and about Rico and Maria being mother and son. And then she ran through everything Maria had told her about Rico.

Swinging her legs out of bed, she poured herself a glass of water. Rico had set out on a mission to reclaim his inheritance, to preserve everything he believed in, just as she had. They had both succeeded. They were both proud and defensive—you had to be when you'd fought so hard for something. She always felt as if everything she had achieved might slip through her fingers if she didn't hold on tight enough.

Zoë's glance grazed the telephone sitting next to her on the bedside table. She had to decide whether to call him or not. Of course she didn't have to do anything—she could just let him slip away into the past...

Zoë was surprised when the operator found the number so easily. She had imagined Rico would have a number that would be withheld from the public. Instead a cultured voice answered her in Spanish right away. It wasn't Rico's voice, it was some other man—his butler, perhaps. She gave her name, and he asked her to wait and he would see whether it was convenient for Señor Alarico to take her call.

It felt like for ever before Rico came on the line, and then he sounded as if he had been exercising. It was a big house,

Zoë reminded herself, with acres of floor space. 'I'm sorry to trouble you.'

'It is no trouble. What can I do for you?'

'Did I disturb you? Were you sleeping?'

'Sleeping? No. I was in the pool—they had to come and get me.'

'I see. I'm sorry,' she said again.

'Don't be.'

The line went quiet as if he was waiting for her to speak. She couldn't change her mind now. 'We didn't finish our conversation earlier.'

Now it was Zoë's turn to wait, not daring to breathe in case she missed his reply.

'I'll come over tomorrow.'

It was less than she had hoped for, but more in some ways. They were speaking at least.

'Or would you prefer to come here?'

Space from the film crew would be good. They were so defensive on her behalf. She loved them for it, but it made any private discussion with Rico impossible. 'I'm going to see Maria—your mother—in the morning.' She was thinking aloud, planning her day.

'Then I'll pick you up around nine. We'll go and see her together. You can come back here for lunch afterwards...if you like?'

'I would like that.' She smiled. 'Nine o'clock, then.'

'See you tomorrow, Zoë.'

The line was cut before she could reply.

Maria couldn't have made it more obvious that she was pleased to see them. She was already up and about, and insisted on making coffee.

'I'm not an invalid,' she told Rico, brushing off his offer to help. 'And before you say a word, I am returning to teaching today.'

'I forbid it—'

'Oh, you do? Do I dance on my hands, Rico? I still have one good hand with which to direct proceedings. And,' she said, refusing to listen to his argument, 'I am to be collected in half an hour. Before I leave, I have something for you, Zoë—to make sure you never stop dancing.'

'I can't possibly take that!' Zoë looked at the lilac dress Maria was holding up. The one she had worn for her first flamenco lesson. 'It must be worth a fortune.'

'It's worth far more than that,' Maria assured her as she pressed it into Zoë's hands. 'And I want you to have it.'

'It's so beautiful,' Zoë said, resting her face against it.

'Yes, it is—and if you ever need a boost, Zoë, you just look at it and think of us.'

'I'll only need to think of you, Maria,' Zoë said, smiling as she hugged Rico's mother.

It was fortunate Zoë couldn't see his mother's imperative drawing together of her upswept black brows, or the fierce command in her eyes, Rico realised as he took the cue to go, and take Zoë with him. 'We'd better leave you now so that you can get ready for your class, Mother.'

'Yes,' Maria said firmly, clearly relieved that her silent message had been understood. 'But before you go, Rico, you can do one more thing for me.'

'What's that?' he said, pausing with his hand on the door.

'Take this with you,' she said, handing him a camera. 'I want a photograph of Zoë in that dress—to hang in the mountain lodge at the flamenco camp,' she explained to Zoë. 'Then I will be able to see the dress and you, Zoë, any time I want.'

Alongside Beba? Immediately Zoë regretted the thought. Maria just wasn't like that. 'I'm sure you don't want reminding of my pathetic efforts—'

'I most certainly do. You were very good—full of genuine passion,' Maria said firmly. 'Now, take this girl to lunch,

Rico. She looks half starved. And don't forget my photograph.'

'I won't,' he promised, sweeping her into his arms for a parting embrace.

Zoë had her hand stuck up her back when she emerged from Rico's dressing-room. He was sitting on the shady veranda at his beach house, where they had been having lunch. He stood as she approached.

'I can't seem to get the dress right—can you help me?' Maria had been on hand the last time to finish off the fastenings for her.

The setting was superb. There was an archway coated in cerise bougainvillea where she would stand for Maria's photograph, with the sea behind her and some flamenco music playing softly to put her in the mood.

Giving up on the dress, Zoë straightened up. 'Help?' she prompted softly.

'Yes, of course.'

Lunch had been a neutral, emotion-free affair, with delicious food served at a leisurely pace, prepared for them by one of Rico's excellent chefs. Zoë knew they were starting again. They were taking it slowly—each of them feeling their way, each of them strangers to love, each of them determined to put at least a toe in the water.

Rico couldn't have planned anything better than this, Zoë thought as she waited for him to finish fastening her dress. It was a treat just to eat food someone else had prepared. Before she met Rico, she had always taken charge of things in the kitchen. He was right: it was good to kick back and relax from time to time.

'Te gusta el flamenco, señorita?'

''*Sí, señor,* I like flamenco very much,' Zoë whispered, trying not to respond to the closeness of his body or the tone of his voice as he reached around her waist to secure the fastenings. Then he murmured, 'Turn around,' and it was impossible, because the warmth of his breath was making every tiny hair on the back of her neck stand erect.

'There—that's done,' he said.

She must have turned too quickly. One silk shoulder strap slipped from her shoulder, and as she went to pull it up again their fingers tangled.

'I'm sorry.' Zoë quickly removed her hand.

'Sorry? What are you sorry for, Zoë?'

His voice was neutral, but his eyes… They were very, very close. His hands were still resting lightly on her waist. 'I didn't give you the chance to explain anything. I just poured out all my own troubles.'

'Stop.' Rico's voice was low, but firm. 'You make it sound as if what happened to you was normal. It wasn't normal, Zoë—and you must never think of it that way or you will come to accept it as normal. You were brutalised—your mind, your body—'

'But I'm all right now.'

'And I'm going to make sure you stay that way.'

'You—'

Rico didn't plan on long explanations. He kissed her so tenderly he made her cry, and he had to catch the tears on her cheeks with his fingertips.

'I feel such a fool.'

'No, you don't,' he assured her. 'You feel wonderful to me.' And, sweeping her into his arms, he walked back into the house.

'What a shame we must take this dress off again,' he said when they reached his bedroom, 'when you have only just put it on.'

He was already halfway down the fastenings as she lay in his arms on the bed. 'Maria's photograph—' Zoë tensed as the last one came free.

'Later.' Rico kissed her shoulder, moving on to nudge her hair aside and kiss her neck.

'But it will be dark later.'

'You will look beautiful by moonlight.'

And then the silk dress was hanging off, and, feeling self-conscious, she wriggled out of it.

Picking it up, Rico tossed it onto a chair by the side of the bed. She wore little underneath it—just a flimsy scrap of a lace thong, not even a bra. There was support built in to the bodice of the dress.

Rico planted kisses as he freed the buttons on his shirt. That followed the dress, and when he kissed her again, and she felt his warm, hard body against her own, Zoë whimpered; she couldn't help herself.

He rested her back against silk and satin, and the linen sheets beneath the covers were scented with lavender. Everything was contrived to please the senses—and it was so easy to slide a little deeper into pleasure beneath his touch.

As Rico looked at the small, pale hands clutching his shoulders, and heard Zoë call his name, he knew she was everything he wanted. Her breasts were so lush, so provocative, the taut nipples reaching out to him, pink and damp where he had tormented her. Her legs moved rhythmically over the bed as she groaned out her need, and now there was just the scrap of lace dissecting the golden tan of her thighs between them.

His gaze swooped up again, lingering on the dark shadow of her cleavage, so deep and lovely. He longed to lose himself in it, to bury his tongue and more besides in its warm, clinging silkiness. But it wasn't just her beauty that bewitched him. He needed her. He had never needed anyone in his life before—he'd made sure of it. But Zoë was different—*he* was different when he was with her, and perhaps that was the most important thing of all.

He watched as she freed the tiny thong and inched it down over her thighs. Had he ever been so aroused? Clamouring sensations gnawed at his control, but he held back. Her trust was too hard won to risk now. How could anyone have abused her? Her skin was as soft and as fragile as the silk upon which she lay. Her eyes were darkening with growing confidence and her lips were parted in invitation. As their eyes locked and she reaffirmed her faith in him, he knew he would defend her with his life.

'Rico…'

As she breathed his name he remembered wryly that foreplay was intended to be an aphrodisiac, not a torture.

He went to pull off the rest of his clothes, but she stopped him. He drew in a deep shuddering breath. He would stop even now if she asked him to.

Scrambling into a sitting position, she touched the belt buckle on his trousers. 'You'll have to help me—my hands are shaking.'

Taking both her hands in his, he kissed each one of her fingertips in turn and then, turning her hands over, planted a tender kiss on each palm.

When Rico finally stood naked before her, Zoë's breath caught in her throat. He was totally unabashed, his dark gaze steady on her face. A lasso of moonlight fell across him, showing the power in his forearms and the wide spread of shoulders. She saw now that his broad chest was shaded with dark hair that tapered down to a hard belly, below which…

She stared into his face, waiting for him to come to her.

Her perfume was intoxicating, drawing him towards her. He stretched his length against her on the bed, not touching her, still holding back. Inhaling deeply, he stroked her thick, silky hair, sifting it through his fingers and enjoying the texture. He loved the way she quivered beneath his touch, eyes closed, mouth slightly open, her breathing nothing more than whispery puffs.

'Rico—'

He kissed her lightly on the lips.

'Kiss me properly.'

'Properly? What do you mean?' His restraint was making her bloom beneath him like a flower that had been too long out of the sun. Her breasts, two perfect globes, were thrust towards him, and her nipples, cruelly neglected, were almost painfully erect. The soft swell of her belly led his gaze down to where she was aching for his attention. Cupping her breasts, he made her gasp. And that gasp soon turned to a whimper as he began to chafe each perfect nipple with his firm thumb pads.

The pleasure was so intense it was almost a pain. He had forgotten how exquisite she was, how sweetly scented, how tender she felt beneath his lips. As he suckled and tugged, and heard her cry out his name, he knew that all he wanted in the world was to keep her safe and love her.

CHAPTER TWELVE

IT WAS so pleasurable, so seductive and intoxicating, fear never entered her head. Zoë wanted to beg Rico to hurry when his firm touch reached her thighs. She had never been so aroused. She cried out with pleasure when his searching fingers finally moved between her legs, and then she begged him not to stop.

Reaching for him, she found she needed two hands to properly encompass him, and he groaned softly beneath her questing fingers until at last she was forced to lift her hands away. Dropping a kiss on her lips, he probed deeply with his tongue, and she pressed against him, searching for the firmer contact she needed so badly.

'Not yet—be patient, *querida*...'

Lifting Zoë's arms above her head, Rico drew her underneath him. As one powerful thigh moved between her legs she shuddered with desire.

'Open your eyes, and look at me, Zoë.'

It was the most exquisite pleasure Zoë had ever known, and the warm, insistent pressure took her to a place where she could only breathe and feel. And then he caught the tip inside her, and it was she who swarmed down the bed to take him deeper. It was so easy, so right, there wasn't a moment of fear or the hint of a painful spasm to wipe out that pleasure.

The pain she had always felt before had been caused by fear, Zoë realised. She wasn't frigid at all. She was just a normal woman who had been waiting for a normal man. And all she wanted now was that Rico took full possession of her body and filled her completely.

She loved this new sensation, the stretching, filling, pulsing.

They started moving together, oblivious to the hungry sounds that escaped their lips, moving firmly until Zoë's fingers bit into the firm flesh of Rico's shoulders and she gave herself up completely to pleasure.

He held her in his arms, stroking her until she was quiet again, and then turned her so that now she was on top of him, straddling him, her legs widely parted. Sweeping the curve of her buttocks with a feathery touch, he tantalised her until she squirmed with delight and longed for him to drag her to him, plunge his tongue deep into the warm secret places of her mouth. But he had more skill than that, and made her wait until she was intoxicated by the raw power burning beneath her.

Feeling the insistent pressure of Rico's erection, Zoë took him deep inside her until she was completely filled. Then she began to move slowly, backwards and forwards, until she felt him take over. Throwing back her head, she closed her eyes, losing herself in sensation while he claimed her breasts, agitating her nipples between thumb and finger until she groaned out her pleasure and begged him for more. He turned her again, bringing her beneath him and using a few firm thrusts to bring on an electrifying climax that went on endlessly until she fell back panting on the bed.

Every part of her was glowing pink in the stunning aftermath of pleasure, Zoë realised, laughing softly with happiness. She had not thought it possible that a man could give himself to a woman so unselfishly. The expression on Rico's face was a fierce mix of passion and tenderness. It made her want him more than ever. She wanted to be the only woman who could put that expression on his face. She wanted his warmth and his strength curled around her for ever. She wanted everything.

As she murmured his name and reached out to him he dragged her close. His drugging kisses, the seductive touch of his hard body was more tantalising than anything she had ever imagined. He knew how to play her, to gently tease her and build her confidence. It was as if they had all the time in the world, and he meant to devote every moment of that time to pleasing her.

His hands were skilled, the look in his eyes commanding. He could order her to new heights of pleasure and she would obey at once. As she enjoyed his warm musky scent, laced with cinnamon and juniper, she felt as if her bones had turned to molten liquid. Her legs moved restlessly on the bed, seeking a cool place and then wrapping around him so he could be in no doubt as to what she wanted.

A great pulse was throbbing between her legs, and yet still he toyed with her, teasing and tempting until she could think of nothing but his firm touch. He must thrust inside her again to the hilt, stretching her wide— 'Please, Rico!'

'So you have not had enough yet?' He sounded pleased.

'Not nearly enough.' She didn't care what he thought of her; all she knew was her need for him. 'Please.'

Rico looked at Zoë, writhing beneath him. More pleasure could be gained by testing themselves to the limit. She must wait. He moved now with an agonising lack of speed, holding away from her until at last he consented to catch just inside her.

Her eyes shot open. 'How can you tease me now?'

'Easily.' He smiled. When she gasped with delight, he slowly brushed the velvet tip against her. 'Is this what you want, Zoë?' He slipped one controlling hand beneath her buttocks.

'You know it is.'

'More than anything?' But she didn't hear him now. Her mind was closed to anything as demanding as speech. She only wanted to feel, and be lost in his arms.

It was late by the time Rico took Zoë back to the castle. He still had work to do, and so did she. The sat in the Jeep like two teenagers who had just discovered each other. They kissed and touched as if every moment might be their last.

Parting from Rico was the hardest thing she had ever had to do, Zoë realised as she climbed out of the Jeep and shut the door. She stood motionless in the courtyard until he had driven away, disappeared from sight, and she couldn't even hear the noise of the engine.

But as she turned she felt as if she was walking six feet off the ground. It was as if the world around her had suddenly come into sharp focus and she had only been viewing it through a veil before. *So this is what happiness feels like,* she thought as she turned her face up to the sky.

Hurrying inside, Zoë couldn't keep the smile off her face. She didn't try. She didn't care if the whole world knew about her and Rico. This was love.

There were five Louis Vuitton suitcases lined up neatly at the end of her bed. Frowning as she dipped down to read the labels, Zoë pulled her hand away as the door swung open behind her.

'Can I help you?'

The voice was young and supercilious. High-pitched. The slight accent suggested she was Spanish.

And very beautiful, Zoë discovered when she turned around. Dressed all in red, the young woman was slender, and shorter than Zoë. The tailoring was Chanel, Zoë guessed from the buttons on her suit jacket, and her glossy black hair was arranged high on her head in an immaculate chignon.

She made Zoë felt scruffy in comparison—scruffy and apprehensive. Her heart was thudding heavily in her chest as she tried not to let her imagination get the better of her. She hadn't a clue who the woman could be. They certainly didn't know each other. This was Rico's castle, yet she seemed perfectly at home. Her mouth was pursed with disapproval, and she was doing a good job of making Zoë feel like the intruder. Zoë was conscious of her own tangled hair, still damp from

Rico's shower. Her face had to be glowing from the aftermath of so much lovemaking, and she knew she was under close inspection.

'What are you doing here?'

'I always stay here,' the young woman said confidently. Crossing to the window, she threw it wide open. She fanned herself theatrically and inhaled deeply, as if its previous occupant had somehow polluted the room.

'I'm sorry—have we met?' Walking up to her, Zoë extended a hand in greeting.

'I'm sure we haven't.'

Dark, cold eyes bored into Zoë's. Fingertips were proffered reluctantly. They were cold too.

'Beba Longoria.'

Zoë couldn't have been more shocked, but she hid it as best she could. *The* Beba? This woman looked nothing like the voluptuous young girl in the poster at the mountain hut. Success had stripped away her bloom, replacing it with an edgy tension. Maybe that was a result of having to defend her position against a constant stream of younger rivals. Yet Maria had remained unchanged…

Zoë pulled herself round with difficulty. 'I'm Zoë Chapman.'

'Ah, so you are Zoë Chapman. I hardly recognised you. You look quite different from the way you appear on television—much older.'

Touché, Zoë thought grimly. She tensed as Beba tossed her handbag onto the bed. The sight of the shiny red pouch clipping the edge of her pillows was the last straw. 'I'm sorry you've had all your things brought in here—someone should have told you I'm using this room. But don't worry. I'll have them transferred.'

'Transferred? What are you talking about?'

'To one of the spare rooms.' Zoë smiled helpfully.

'You clearly don't know who I am.'

'I've seen your poster at the mountain hut—'

'Then Rico must have told you.'

'Rico?' Zoë's confident expression faltered. Inwardly she was in crisis. But she had to try not to jump to conclusions. Rico had brothers and sisters. Beba might be one of them. Longoria could be her married name.

'Alarico Cortes? You do know who I'm talking about?'

'Of course I know him.'

'I see.' One perfectly groomed brow lifted as Beba stared at Zoë thoughtfully, and Zoë realised her hasty response had given away too much. She was on the back foot, cheeks blazing, when it should have been Beba feeling the heat.

'There's an understanding between us.' Beba's voice had dropped to a confidential level, as if she was trying to drop a bomb lightly on Zoë's head. 'Rico and I have been together since we were children. I'm surprised he didn't mention you to me—but then I suppose he can't be expected to remember every woman he meets.'

Turning away, she checked her hair in the dressing-table mirror, picking up Zoë's hand mirror to look at the back.

Zoë could feel the hostile black eyes spying on her through the mirror. But she was determined to hold herself together. 'There's obviously been a mistake.' She shrugged, and kept it pleasant. 'You see, I have taken a lease on the castle, and I'm using this suite of rooms during my tenancy. As you haven't unpacked yet, I'll just call down and have one of the crew come up and help you move to another room—'

'That won't be necessary.'

'I don't want to cause you any inconvenience.' Zoë's anger propelled her into action. She was already freeing the handle on the top of one of Beba's suitcases when she spoke again. 'So of course you are welcome to stay at the castle until you find alternative accommodation.'

'Rico will hear about this!'

'I'm afraid he has no legal rights over the castle until my lease expires. I doubt he can help you.'

'Alarico Cortes wields more power than you could ever understand.' Beba's face was twisted in an ugly mask as she snatched up her handbag from the bed. 'When he hears that I have been insulted—'

'He'll what?'

'Throw you onto the street!'

As Beba swept out of the room Zoë sank down on the bed. Her heart was thundering, but her mind was mercifully empty. She was numb with shock. All she was aware of was the click-clack of heels rattling away down the landing towards the main staircase.

When it was silent again, Zoë found she was shuddering uncontrollably. Burying her face in her hands, she drew her feet up on the bed and curled herself into a tight, defensive ball. Had Rico known about this when they were in bed together? Would Beba have dared to march into the castle and throw her weight around unless they were an item, as she said? Rico had never mentioned another woman. But a man like Rico Cortes with no woman in his life? She really had been living in a dream world!

Was she the type of companion El Señor Alarico Cortes de Aragon would take to the court of the King of Spain? Or would he take Beba—glamorous flamenco star? It was a stark choice between a cook with red hands and wild hair, or someone perfectly groomed, someone fragrant and dainty, with long, manicured fingernails and a musical laugh. She was quite certain Beba had a musical laugh.

Zoë reached for the phone and punched in some numbers. Rico's butler told her Señor Cortes was still out on business. No, he didn't know when he would be back. When pressed, the man admitted Señor Cortes was expected to return before a dinner appointment out, later that evening.

Later that evening! She couldn't wait until later that evening. She had to see him now —speak to him right away—resolve all this. There had to be an explanation.

Rico hadn't mentioned any plans for them, Zoë realised as she cut the line. It had never crossed her mind to ask when they would see each other again—she had taken it for granted. She felt sick, faint. She wanted this to be a nightmare. Because if it wasn't, she was on her way to making a fool of herself for the second time in her life.

She couldn't do anything yet, and it was far better to be busy than to brood, Zoë thought, wheeling the last of Beba's suitcases out of her room. She was hot all over again with the effort of lugging five overweight suitcases into position. She had showered and changed into fresh clothes right after Beba left, and now she would have to shower again, and dry and brush her hair until it shone. She had no intention of wearing her heartbreak on her sleeve. Life went on, with or without Rico Cortes. She was just glad to have a job to pour her energies into, as well as people who relied on her to take the helm.

This time when Zoë left her room she locked the door—something she hadn't felt the need to do since she'd moved into the castle. Hurrying downstairs, she found the team busy working on something in the Great Hall.

Philip swung round when he heard her.

'What's going on?' Zoë could see he was in one of his excitable moods. 'Well, are you going to tell me?' she said, smiling at him as she watched him picking his way over some camera cables.

'Cazulas is one incredible place, Zoë. You won't believe who has turned up now.'

Oh, yes, she would! 'Try me.'

'Only Beba! The best flamenco dancer in all of Spain.'

'Maria is the best flamenco dancer in all of Spain.'

'You know this Beba chick?'

'I've heard of her.'

'Well, you could sound a little more excited.'

'We haven't discussed another feature, Philip,' Zoë said, frowning as she realised what he planned to do.

'What about replacing that footage we didn't like? It's too good an opportunity to miss. Come on, Zoë. We could make this the last and best show of the series.'

He was right. 'So what's the angle? We already have the best flamenco dancer in Spain. That's how we billed Maria.'

'Beba appeals to the youngsters. She's like a pop star in the Latin world. We're talking glamour, we're talking riches, we're talking one sassy lady.'

'Yes, thank you. I think I get the picture.'

'But you haven't heard it all yet. Our audience get Beba— and then you remind the viewers about Maria, the greatest flamenco dancer in Spain! She's agreed to come for the filming, by the way—the old and the new, two for the price of one! What do you say, Zoë?'

'I'd say if I was Maria I'd be pretty insulted.'

'That's where you come in to it. You write the script and make sure she isn't insulted.'

'I can see you've got it all worked out, Philip—but after I write the script what will I cook? You do remember this is a cookery series?'

'Stop worrying, Zoë. I've got it all worked out. We're going to have a café-style setting, with a fabulous selection of food.'

'I see. And where are the ingredients coming from for this fabulous selection of food? And who is going to eat it all?'

'There's a vanload of produce arriving any time now. Come on, Zoë, don't be difficult.'

The thought of having Beba under the same roof for a moment longer than necessary didn't appeal—and Zoë wasn't happy about casual arrangements for food she hadn't picked out herself. But if she agreed she would be so frantically busy there would be no time to think about her personal problems...

'The girls have been round the village already, and everyone is keen to come back and act as extras for the programme, so we have our audience.'

'I do have some stock in the deep-freeze...'

'Don't get hung up on minor details, Zoë. This is going to be a sensational programme and you know it.'

'Food is a pretty large "minor detail" on a cookery show,' Zoë pointed out dryly. But it would prove to Beba—and Rico?—that she had bounced back without causing more than a ripple in her everyday schedule if she could pull it off. 'OK, I'll do it.' And then something else occurred to her. 'Was it you who installed Beba in my bedroom?'

'No, of course not. I didn't even know she had done that.'

His shock was genuine, Zoë realised. 'Don't worry, I moved her out. But you had better see she gets a nice suite of rooms if you want her happy for the programme.'

'She'll have the best.'

'No—I've already got that,' Zoë said, savouring her one small victory. She was starting to fire with enthusiasm. She always did for a new programme. 'I'll need some quiet time to work on the script, then I can get on to the food. When are we filming?'

'Tonight.'

'Tonight!' Get over it, Zoë thought. True, it didn't give her much time. But if they were filming, and Beba was dancing, Beba couldn't be with Rico. That suited her. And if Beba could dance as well as everyone said, it would make great television...

Zoë worked on her script in the bedroom, where she knew she would be undisturbed. She had one call from Philip, to warn her that Beba had insisted on complete artistic control over her performance. Zoë was happy to give it to her. The film would be edited before it was shown. Philip also told her that Beba was now happily installed in one of the grandest suites at the castle. Zoë was relieved to hear she was keeping a low profile, and had been most co-operative. One less thing to worry about, she thought with relief, replacing the receiver.

By the time the food was ready Zoë had to admit the team had done a great job. The Great Hall looked magical. Jewel-coloured tapestries and Persian rugs glowed in the candlelight, and there were colourful floral displays everywhere.

The setting was that of an intimate cellar club, with café tables arranged in groups around a circular wooden stage. People from the village had started to arrive, and were already being shown to their places. Zoë smiled with anticipation. She couldn't help it. This tense air of anticipation for the unexpected was what had drawn her to television in the first place.

But Rico was always there in her mind.

The worry, the uncertainty about him didn't go away. There had still been no word from him. She had tried telling herself it didn't matter, but that was a lie. All she wanted was for him to walk in now, walk up to her, take her in his arms and tell her she had nothing to worry about—that Beba meant nothing to him and never had.

There was no sign of Beba either.

People smiled, and she smiled back, but concern was nagging away at her. He should have been in contact by now. He drove too fast. Surely he hadn't had an accident?

Zoë spun round as the door opened. 'Maria! I'm so pleased you agreed to come.'

'I wouldn't miss this night for the world.'

'Have you seen Rico?'

'No.' She looked at Zoë with concern.

'I'm sorry, Maria, I'm sure he'll be along later. How's your arm?'

'Sore, but mending. I don't need the sling now, and I took the bandage off.'

'That's good.' Zoë could see Maria felt her agitation. So

much for not brandishing her private concerns in public! 'You are dancing tonight? I'm sorry it's such short notice…'

As Maria touched her arm she smiled warmly into Zoë's eyes. 'Maybe I will have the chance to dance with you, Zoë?'

I hope not—for the sake of the audience, Zoë thought wryly—though even that, whether she bodged it or not, would make good television. 'Do you know Beba well?' she said, returning to the subject uppermost in her mind.

'Beba?' Maria paused. 'Yes, I know Beba.'

'Was she always so friendly with Rico?'

'You know about that?'

Zoë's heart plummeted. Time to act her socks off. But they were standing very close, and Maria was very shrewd. 'Yes, Rico told me all about it. They make a handsome couple.'

'You do know that she used to be my pupil?'

'Your pupil?' Of course. It all made sense now. 'I saw the poster at the mountain hut.'

'My most celebrated pupil.' There was an odd expression on Maria's face.

'I see.'

'No, you don't,' Maria assured her, patting Zoë's cheek.

'Is she with Rico now?'

'It would not surprise me.'

Zoë couldn't stop now. 'Have you seen them together here at the castle—tonight?'

'Stop worrying, Zoë,' Maria said gently. 'Rico will be here. He will not let you down.'

He already had, Zoë thought.

Her legs felt like lumps of lead as she showed Maria to her table at the front of the stage. She felt sick and light-headed; there were icy cramps in her stomach. She really had no idea how she was going to get through the rest of the evening. But then the floor manager beckoned to her urgently. She welcomed the distraction. Work had always proved a refuge. Quite soon Wardrobe and Make-up would want her too, and she still had to make a crucial addition to her script to explain that Beba had been Maria's star pupil. The news couldn't have come at a more useful time. As far as the show went, Zoë reflected dryly, it couldn't have worked out any better.

Half an hour later the cameras were ready to roll. The main lights had been switched off, and apart from the necessary television lights the only illumination now came from candle-light. It was the most romantic setting imaginable. But as Zoë stood waiting for her cue to introduce Beba she was sure her heart had shrivelled to the size of a nutmeg.

Her sights were firmly fixed on the single spotlight trained on the main entrance. The guitarist was already seated on his stool, and at any moment Beba would appear.

She started when the *tio* from the village touched her arm. She didn't want to offend him by pointing out that the red light would flash on at any second.

'You look worried.' He frowned.

'Always am just before we start recording,' Zoë explained in a whisper. 'Maria's saving you a seat at the front.'

Worried? Concern was eating her up inside. *Was Rico with Beba? How could Rico be with Beba?* The two thoughts were spinning in her mind until she thought she would go mad.

'You must be looking forward to seeing Beba dance?'

'She is a fine dancer.'

Zoë wondered at the *tio's* lack of enthusiasm for the local star. Maria had taught Beba to dance, so surely Beba's success reflected well on Cazulas as well as on her teacher?

A sudden sound made Zoë jump, and with another light touch to her arm the *tio* was gone. Preparing to do her voice-over, Zoë realised the sound she had heard was the rattle of castanets, played by an expert.

There was one more imperative tattoo, and then, wearing a scarlet dress so tight it might have been painted onto her naked body, Beba stepped into the spotlight—on the arm of Rico Cortes.

CHAPTER THIRTEEN

SHE couldn't break down. Not here—not with everyone to see. Zoë forced her concentration on to the small performance area and cleared her mind of everything but the music—that and her commentary between the various dances.

Beba danced with such purpose, such certainty, it made Zoë shiver. It was as if the young flamenco dancer siphoned up energy from the music and spat it out again in furious movement. Her stabbing heels beat faster than a hummingbird's wings, and there was such passion in her dance that inwardly Zoë recoiled from it. The swirling skirts of Beba's tight scarlet dress shattered the air into smothering perfumed waves.

The dance ended on a crashing chord. The proud head tilted down and Beba's fierce black stare found Zoë's face. At the same moment Zoë knew Rico was making his way discreetly around the back of the hall towards her. After a brief moment of silence the thunderous applause came. She took the chance to move away, but someone caught hold of her arm.

'Maria!' Looking round, Zoë saw the *tio* was talking to Rico. They were trying to hold a conversation above the cheers, the shouts and the stamping feet—the *tio* had his hand cupped to his ear.

'Do you hear that?' Maria whispered in her ear.

How could she not? Zoë thought, forcing a smile. The noise was deafening.

'Do you hear *duende*?' Maria persisted.

'No,' Zoë admitted. She could hear, *'Olé! Brava! Eso es!'*

She really wanted to go. She couldn't bear this any longer. What difference could one word make?

'Now you will hear *duende*!' Maria's voice was commanding as she thrust the beautiful lilac dress she had been holding over her arm into Zoë's hands.

'Are you mad?' Zoë looked down at it in amazement. 'I could never follow that.'

'I can.' Maria's eyes were twinkling again. 'Let us go now, and change into our performance clothes.'

'No!'

'Would you let me down, Zoë? Would you?' she said again, when Zoë remained silent. 'I have told your director; he knows all about this. He says it will be the perfect final sequence for your series.'

Zoë shook her head, thinking of Rico and how he would view her dancing right after Beba's spectacular display. She felt bad enough about the situation. How much humiliation could she take? 'No, Maria. I don't want to let you down, but I can't do it.'

'Yes, you can,' Maria insisted fiercely. 'Whatever happens on that stage, it will make good television.'

'Maria, please—'

'And I need you to help me into my dress. My arm, as I already told you, is still a little sore...'

Zoë made a sound of despair. She couldn't refuse. And now the *tio* had finished talking to Rico, and he was making fast progress around the hall towards her. 'All right,' she agreed tensely. 'I just hope you know what you are doing.'

'Of course I do,' Maria said firmly, pushing Zoë in front of her with her good arm.

Zoë would never know quite what happened on stage that night. She only knew that concern for Maria took her there, and the thought of how Rico had betrayed her supplied the passion.

Maria performed as she always did as if she had absorbed the emotional energy of every person in the audience and released it in breathtakingly fluid moves, and by the time the finale came Zoë hardly cared that Beba had joined them on stage.

'Do you hear it now?' Maria whispered in Zoë's ear.

Zoë listened. She had been so absorbed in her dancing she was hardly aware that it had come to an end, and that now the three of them were standing side by side, acknowledging the gratitude of the audience.

The cries of *'Duende!'* were coming from all around her, Zoë realised incredulously. She could hardly believe it, and then Rico was on stage too, and her mind was reeling as he seized her hands and raised them to his lips.

'You did it, Zoë! You did it!'

He seemed pleased…even proud. And he looked so handsome, with his seductive mouth curving into a grin. She couldn't bear it, and turned her face away. But he cupped her chin and brought her back so she had nowhere to look but into his eyes.

'You have just earned the ultimate accolade in the world of flamenco, Señorita Chapman.' Then he raised her arm and the crowd went wild.

Why didn't you tell me about Beba? Why didn't you warn me? Why did you make love to me when you knew she would be here? Was I just something to fill a gap in your schedule before you had to meet her?

All Zoë's pleasure had drained away. She was like a rag doll, limp and unresponsive. Rico hadn't noticed. He was already moving away from her to embrace his mother. Then finally he took Beba's hand, and Zoë saw the way the dancer looked at him, her dark eyes shining with adoration as he raised her arm in a victory salute.

As another great roar went up Zoë felt her eyes fill with tears. She hated herself for the weakness and could think of nothing but getting away—out of the spotlight, out of Cazulas, and out of Spain. Everyone was happy to see Rico and Beba together again—of course they were. And she was a fool if she thought El Señor Alarico Cortes would choose a cook over his very beautiful, very gifted fiancée.

She could never stand by and see the man she loved with another woman at his side. She had built a new life, won back her self-respect. Making herself available whenever Rico had an itch to scratch was not for her. Smiling brightly at the cameras for the last time, Zoë seized the chance to slip away.

When the knocking started up on her bedroom door, Zoë clutched the sheet to her chest and stayed motionless, listening.

'Zoë, it's me,' Rico called to reassure her. 'Open the door.'

She tensed. Was Beba with him? No—even Rico would not go that far. But Maria was right; the Cortes family did move in sophisticated circles. Rico might think they could make love all day, and again at night, with Beba sandwiched in between. She would not open the door, no matter how much he knocked...

But he didn't knock again. Zoë frowned. She couldn't help but be disappointed that he had given up so fast.

She turned to the window. 'Rico!'

'You should lock these doors at night,' he said, stepping into the room from the balcony.

'I always do.'

'Well, tonight you forgot.'

Instinct made her gaze past him, just to make sure he was alone.

'Who are you expecting?' he said quizzically.

'I didn't think Beba would want to be left alone.'

'Beba is never alone.' Rico laughed as he bent to switch on the light.

'Do you mind? I'm asleep.'

'No, you're not—unless you talk in your sleep.' He smiled as he sat down beside her.

'What do you think you're doing?'

'I'm taking my shoes off. I don't usually wear them in bed.'

'You're not getting into bed with me!'

'Why not?'

'Rico. I can't—'

'You can't what, Zoë?' He brushed a strand of hair back from her face. 'I thought we'd got past this.'

Even though every fibre of her being was filled with longing she pushed his hand away. 'Please—don't.'

'What's happened, Zoë?'

'Beba happened.'

'Beba?'

'You went to her after you slept with me.'

'She wanted to see me.'

'You don't even bother to deny it?' Zoë stopped. She could hear the hysteria rising in her voice.

'No. Why should I?'

This wasn't how it was supposed to be. She had intended to be brisk and to the point, to confront him with facts, hear him out, and then tell him to go. But life was never that clearcut, or that simple. She should have known. 'I can't do this, Rico—this is never going to work for me.'

'What isn't going to work for you, Zoë? Are you afraid of me? Is that why you're pushing me away?'

She *was* afraid of him, but not in the way he thought. She didn't have what it took to sustain a relationship. A career, yes—she had proved that—but for some reason it seemed she wasn't meant to find happiness with a man. 'I can't believe you misled me again, Rico.'

'About Beba?' He stood up and looked down at her, the proud angles of his face harshly etched in the lamplight.

'She told me—'

'She told you what?'

'That you and she were an item.'

'Then she lied.'

'You never cared for each other?'

'I didn't say that.'

Zoë didn't want to hear any more; she couldn't bear to. 'If you'll excuse me,' she mumbled. Swinging her legs over the opposite side of the bed, she hurried to the bathroom. She closed the door and leaned back against it. Everything she had rebuilt before coming to Spain was in danger of collapsing, thanks to Rico.

But when she had calmed down a little she knew the answer didn't lie in hiding away from him. Grabbing her robe down from the back of the door, she threw it on, belting it tightly. She went into the bedroom again, and switched on the main light.

'Sit down, Rico.' She pointed to the elegant sofa positioned to take in the view from the balcony. 'We really need to get everything out in the open.'

'I'm all right—you sit down. You've had quite a night.'

She searched his face for irony; there was none. 'You can't have us both, Rico.' Standing stiffly, facing him, Zoë raked her hair until it stood around her head like a wild golden-red nimbus.

Rico's gaze never wavered. 'I don't want anyone but you, Zoë.'

How she wanted to believe him. How she wanted to close the small gap between them, throw her arms around his neck and tell him she would stay with him for ever, and under any circumstances. But that would only lead to bitterness and resentment in the end.

'Is there an understanding between the two of you?'

'There was.'

Spain was a traditional country; this was a very traditional part of Spain. Zoë couldn't imagine such 'understandings' were embarked upon lightly.

'I can see you must need an appropriate wife…'

Yes, he had thought that at one time, Rico remembered. When he was younger. When he'd made his first fortune he had been brim-full of arrogance—partly because he hadn't been sure what was expected of a young aristocrat with a huge amount of money in the bank. Now he realised it didn't matter how much money you had, or what your title was. The only thing that mattered was that you made your corner of the world a little better. His mother Maria had done that, without a fortune or a title, and she was his only benchmark for success.

'I don't *need* a wife at all. Do you want me to tell you what Beba's doing at the castle?'

Suddenly she wasn't sure that she did, Zoë realised. If she was going to leave Spain in one piece emotionally, she didn't want to hear another word. In fact, this was the moment she should tell Rico to get lost.

He didn't give her that option. In a couple of strides he had her arms in his grasp. 'I listened to you, Zoë, and now it's your turn to listen to me.'

Zoë tensed. Rico's gaze was frightening in its intensity.

'Or are you just too scared to risk your heart again?'

Scared? She was scared of nothing. She stopped fighting him and clenched her jaw.

'You've built walls so high around you, Zoë, you can't see what's happening outside your own stockade.'

'That's not true!'

'Isn't it? Oh, you're safe enough in there, but you're not going to have much of a life.'

'Just tell me this—are you engaged to Beba?'

'Beba was my fiancée.'

'Was?' Zoë made a short humourless sound. 'She certainly didn't give me the impression she was in the past tense. Oh, I'm glad you can smile about it!'

'I can smile where Beba's concerned—that's just the point. She doesn't change. That's why we're not together now—whatever she might think, or might have told you.'

'So what is the position between you? Did she just turn up

in Cazulas out of the blue—to help me make a television programme, perhaps?'

He ignored her sarcasm. 'Beba? Helping others? That's more in your line, Zoë. Beba was the star in my mother's dance class. We became lovers around the same time I heard I was going to inherit my father's title.'

'Do you think that was a coincidence?'

'I don't think anything is a coincidence where Beba is concerned. I was young, and I thought we were in love. I thought we loved each other. Then Beba discovered that my inheritance was just a title and nothing more—no money, no castle. She hadn't expected that. I explained that it was only a matter of time before I rebuilt the family fortune, but she couldn't wait. I can't blame her. She had talent. She could earn her own money. I was all fired up. It never occurred to me that Beba might not share my enthusiasm for the long years of poverty that lay ahead. She broke off our engagement and went to Madrid to seek her fortune.'

'Which she found,' Zoë murmured.

'I never wanted to hold her back, and I'm delighted that she has been so successful. I was equally determined that I would earn the right to be called El Señor Alarico Cortes de Aragon.'

'Which you did.'

'Yes.'

'And now Beba has returned to Cazulas for the one thing she doesn't have yet, and that's you.'

'Another trophy to add to the others.' Rico smiled wryly at her. 'I would have explained all this to you if I'd known what Beba planned to do in advance, and if my business meeting hadn't gone on for so long. When I arrived at the castle and found she was here it was already too late.'

'But you met with her?'

'I had to talk to her. I had to tell her how I feel about you.'

'About me?'

There was no such thing as dipping your toe in the water with Rico. It was total immersion or nothing. It was the sort of commitment Zoë feared above anything else. Staying safe inside her stockade, as Rico put it, had kept her sane since her divorce. The closest she had ever come to letting go was with him, and she didn't know if she had what it took to let go completely.

'It was only right to escort Beba onto the stage when she asked me to,' Rico went on. 'I knew that playing the tragic heroine suited her purpose. That sort of thing always puts her in the right mood for the dance. But I have no ambition to become an emotional punch-bag. She's just not my type of woman.'

'Are you sure about that?'

'Of course I'm sure. Didn't you notice all that anger and aggression? It has to come from somewhere, Zoë. Beba uses people. She sucks them dry and spits them out—they're just the fuel for her dance.'

'You make her sound so callous.'

'So lonely. That's why she came here to find me—to see if there was any chance of us getting together again.'

'And you refused her?'

'Of course I refused her. Beba and I don't love each other—we never did. I asked her to marry me because I thought I should, and she agreed to marry me—well, you know why. Circumstances pushed us together when we were too young to know any better, but we each had our own very different road to travel.'

'And now those roads have crossed again?'

'I want a wife who will travel the same road as me, Zoë. I don't want a woman who is trawling the world in search of the next thrill.'

'But if Beba had been different?'

Shaking his head, Rico gave a wry smile. 'Beba couldn't be different. Beba couldn't be you.'

'And Cazulas was too small to hold her?'

'The world is too small to contain Beba. She's only here now because she is in between tours. She feeds on drama. The stage, a new lover—it's all the same to her. There is no doubt in my mind at all, Zoë. It's you I want.'

Foreboding coloured everything Zoë was hearing—everything Rico was saying to her. El Señor Alarico Cortes would one day want a suitable wife—not one who travelled the world to pursue her own career. When that day arrived would she be expected to stand aside and spend the rest of her life in the shadows? Rico's father had been a Spanish grandee too. He'd given Maria the flamenco dancer a son, but hadn't married her. Was that par for the course? Was his proud, complex son now offering her his love along with the promise of future pain? Was that what she wanted? Passion with all the heat of flamenco that would burn itself out until it only existed in her memory like a few fast-fading chords?

'Won't you come downstairs to join the party?' Rico pressed, relaxing now he believed he had set everything straight. 'Maria and the *tio* are waiting to see you—to congratulate you on your success.'

It was the end of an intensive stretch of work for the crew. It was churlish of her to stay in her room. Rico didn't need to know that her mind was made up: she was leaving Cazulas for good.

Zoë actually flinched as the thought hovering in her mind became reality. Just outing it gave it clarity, gave it purpose, set it in stone. It was easier than she had imagined. She *was* leaving Cazulas for good. And not because she didn't believe Rico about Beba, but because she did. He really loved her, he really wanted her; she could see that now. But she had nothing to offer him in return. She didn't have anything left inside her. She didn't have the courage it took to risk her heart again, to risk the pain he could cause her. She had been safe feeling nothing...

'Zoë, look at me—don't shut me out.'

The look in Rico's eyes was so intense she felt dizzy, bewildered, disorientated. And then he took her hand and she felt the power he wielded, the force of his will, his strength, his passion flooding into her.

Escape for one more night. Physical pleasure so intense she could shut off the part of her that knew there must be consequences—Rico could offer her that. They could have one last night together, and then she would retreat inside that stockade he'd talked about—her stockade, where not even the memory of their affair would be able to reach her.

'If I put on the lilac dress again, would you take that photograph for Maria?'

'You know I will. Shall I wait outside while you change your clothes?'

'Do you mind?'

'Not at all.'

Zoë watched Rico until he left the room. After all the intimacy they'd shared it seemed bizarre to have such reserve spring up between them now. He respected her, and if she had been content to be his mistress without having to give her love she had no doubt he would have protected her. But it wasn't nearly enough.

When she was ready, Rico escorted Zoë downstairs again.

'I'm wearing the dress so Rico can take that photograph you wanted,' she said when they found Maria.

'You make it sound as if you're leaving us, Zoë.'

There was an expression in Maria's eyes that made Zoë look away. She could lie to herself—she had perfected the art. But she could never lie to Maria.

'Rico.' Beba came over the moment she spotted him. 'We were all wondering where you had got to.'

Her cold dark gaze lingered on Zoë's face, and Zoë was glad when Rico drew her arm through his own.

'I had some important business to attend to,' he said.

'So I see. Well, if you will excuse me…' She turned away, then swung back again. Seizing Zoë's hand, she clasped it in her own. 'I wish you luck.' She slanted a hostile glance at Rico. 'You're going to need it.'

Sour grapes? Zoë wondered. Or sound advice?

She could see the crew already starting to clear up some of the equipment. The hall was emptying fast. Once the series was in the can no one hung around; they had all been away from home too long as it was. She knew they would work through the night if necessary, just to be able to catch the first flight back. She would leave the castle shortly after them, though Rico didn't need to know that.

The arrival of Beba had shaken her. Rico had reassured her where Beba was concerned, but what happened when he wanted a wife? She couldn't give up the independence she had won at so high a price to become a rich man's mistress… But she could have one more night.

'Rico?'

Something in her voice told him what she wanted, and his eyes darkened with desire. 'Are you ready to go to bed now?'

'If you still want me.'

They said their goodnights quickly. And as their fingers intertwined Zoë could think of nothing but the next few hours as Rico led her towards the stairs.

CHAPTER FOURTEEN

Zoë's lips slipped open beneath the gentle pressure of Rico's mouth. Deepening the kiss, he stripped off the lilac dress while his tongue sought out the dark, secret places in her mouth.

It was as if they had never made love before, her hunger for him was so great. He was inside her before they reached the bed with her legs locked around his waist and her arms secured round his neck, her fingers meshed through his hair. He supported her easily, with his strong hands beneath her buttocks, and the reassurance of feeling him hard and deep inside her was almost unbearably good.

She had to remember this moment for a lifetime, Zoë thought, as Rico lowered her onto the edge of the mattress.

They made love there, with no preliminaries and with no thought of seeking the luxury of the well-sprung bed. Zoë cried out her encouragement as Rico tipped her at an angle, resting her legs over his shoulders to increase satisfaction for them both. And all the time he moved inside her he murmured her name, and told her how much he loved her, and how he wanted to be with her for ever...

This was for ever, Zoë thought. For her, at least.

Zoë stopped waving as the last van disappeared out of sight. She could feel her colleagues' hugs still imprinted on her skin, and hear their words of encouragement and good wishes ringing in her ears. None of them knew how she felt inside. They would never know.

Rico had left her at dawn. It really couldn't have worked

out any better. He had some business to attend to back at the beach house, and so she had been spared a painful parting.

She had slept fitfully in his arms all night, dreading the morning, dreading the moment when she would tell him she couldn't stay in Cazulas. Her idea of sleeping with him one last time, making love with him half the night in the hope of keeping the memory alive, had been a terrible mistake. Instead of leaving her with tender memories to carry forward when she left Spain for good, it had left her with guilt and unbearable loss.

She had learned nothing from the past. She was betraying Rico just as she had been betrayed. Her ex-husband had won the final battle now she had completed the circle of violence. There was no physical violence, of course, but she was violating Rico's trust. She had taken his love and was letting it slip through her fingers because she didn't have the guts to hang on to it. She was still scared of commitment, still scared to risk her heart. She was brave enough to take the pleasure now—just not brave enough to take the consequences.

The best thing for Rico, the best thing all round, would be if she left without a fuss. Her suitcases were already packed, and she intended to drive to the station around noon.

It was strange being alone in the castle. Even Beba had packed up and gone, and it was a quiet, lonely place now. She couldn't bear the thought of leaving her friends in the village, but she didn't belong in Cazulas any more than Beba. Her life revolved around a television programme, and it was time to return to reality.

Back in the kitchen, Zoë could hardly bring herself to look at the collection of local pottery on the table. She was taking all of it back to England. She was quite sure Rico wouldn't want any reminders of her visit. The crew had left some empty packing cases for her, and a removal van was due to arrive before she left for the station. All the heavy equipment for the show that wouldn't fit into the vans had to be shipped back to the UK, and the pottery would be delivered to her London home at the same time.

She had been packing and wrapping for some time when she heard the music. Leaving the kitchen, she hurried into the hall.

'Good morning, Zoë.'

'Rico!'

He was sitting cross-legged on a stool in the centre of the floor, one hand caressing the neck of his guitar, the other hovering over the strings. She had thought it would be possible to get used to the idea of living without him, but in that instant Zoë knew she was wrong.

Turning back to his guitar, he started to play again, as if she wasn't there. The music held her transfixed. He stopped playing quite suddenly. His slap on the side of the guitar echoed around the empty hall. Laying the guitar down carefully on the floor, he stood, reminding her how tall he was, how commanding.

'When were you going to tell me you were leaving?'

Zoë stared at him. There was nothing she could say to justify her actions.

'Don't you think you owe me an explanation?'

'I'm sorry—'

'You're *sorry*?' he said incredulously.

'I need my work—'

'And?'

Zoë's voice was barely above a whisper. It was as if she was talking to herself, trying to convince herself and not him. 'I can't let anyone take over my life again.'

'Take over your life? What the hell are you talking about, Zoë?' He made no attempt to close the distance between them.

'It's all I've got. It's what I do.'

'It's all you had,' he said fiercely.

'You don't understand, Rico. I just can't be there for you.'

He turned away, but not before she saw the hurt in his eyes. 'That's different.'

His voice was hoarse, and he didn't look at her when he spoke. They might have been standing on separate ice floes, drifting steadily apart. But this was what she wanted, wasn't it—this final break between them? She just hadn't imagined doing it face to face. In her usual cowardly way she had been going to bury her head in the sand somewhere far away from Spain.

'You can't be there for me?' he repeated bitterly. 'So what was I, Zoë? Some type of experiment? Just a random male you could use to exorcise your ghosts?'

'Don't say that, Rico.'

'Why not? Because it's true?' He laughed, and it was a hard, ugly sound. 'You should be happy.'

'Happy?' Zoë could hear incredulity approaching hysteria in her voice.

'At least you know you're not frigid now.'

'Stop it!' She covered her ears.

'No, you stop it!' Rico said with an angry gesture. 'You come here to Cazulas. You seek help for your show, which I give to you freely. We make love—at least I did. Yes, I love you, Zoë,' he confirmed fiercely. 'But you just used me. You're no better than Beba!'

'Rico!' Through her shock, Zoë knew what he was saying was true. She reached out to him. 'Rico—don't go yet. Can't we talk?'

'Why shouldn't I go? The only reason I can think of for you wanting me to stay is that you need some more reassurance in bed. And frankly, Zoë, I'm not in the mood.'

The stool was kicked over as he snatched up his guitar, and then he went to the door. Halting with his hand on the heavy iron handle, he turned to her. 'You might as well have this.'

Zoë started towards him, but she was too late.

Putting an envelope on the table by the door, he walked out.

The castle was like a deserted shell. There was no life, no sound, nothing. Zoë's footsteps echoed on the stone-flagged floors as she completed her final check. Even the towering walls seemed to have grown cold and unfriendly. She was glad when she finally closed the heavy oak door behind her; an empty castle was a lonely place.

The removal van had taken the last of her things away, and the few bits and pieces she had found now could be loaded into the car. There was nothing for her to stay for. But before she left Cazulas for good there was one more stop she had to make.

Maria ushered her into the cottage. 'It's very good of you to see me,' Zoë said.

'Rico told me you were leaving.'

'Now I'm here, I don't know where to begin...'

'At the beginning?' Maria suggested gently. 'But first you must sit down. You look worn out.'

'No, no, I'm fine.' Rico's face flashed into her mind, and then the contents of the envelope he had left behind. She bit her lip. 'Truthfully, Maria, I'm not fine.'

'I can see that. Come and sit here with me at the fireside. You take this chair across from mine.'

The overhead fan was whirring. It was almost midday. The shutters were closed and it was hot in the small room. But the fireside was a symbol to Zoë—a symbol of Maria's happy, well-ordered life.

And as she talked things through with Maria it was as if Zoë saw everything clearly for the first time. She saw how she was pushing Rico away each time he got close, grabbing at excuses to justify her actions. She understood the bewilderment she had felt at discovering that having the most wonderful sex with him hadn't been enough to exorcise her demons, after all. She had to stop holding back before that could happen, but she was still terrified of risking herself in a relationship again—so terrified she hadn't even paused to consider how Rico might feel.

And now she was ashamed. She was particularly ashamed in front of Maria, who had given so much of herself so generously—to Rico, to his father, and to the village of Cazulas. If Maria hadn't prompted her so gently, encouraged her so warmly, Zoë knew she would never have had the confidence to pour her heart out as she did.

When she had finished, she gave Maria the envelope Rico had left at the castle.

Maria hesitated, holding it in her hands.

'Please read what's inside,' Zoë prompted.

Maria read the papers, and then put them carefully back into the envelope.

'My son must love you very much. Did you doubt him?'

'Before I met Rico I couldn't see beyond what had happened to me in the past.'

'And after you met him?'

Zoë turned away, unable to meet Maria's candid stare.

'Since he inherited his father's title Rico has been prey to fortune hunters and the press. You have a mutual enemy in the paparazzi, Zoë.'

'Yes, I can see that now.'

'Rico was furious when he returned from his travels to discover that his land agent had leased Castillo Cazulas to a television company. But then he fell in love with you—'

'And made me a gift of the castle.'

'Don't look so surprised. He wanted you to have a Spanish headquarters; the castle is perfect. It is far too big for a family home. Imagine what a film set it will make. Rico must have been on the point of asking you to marry him.'

'Marry him? No, you're wrong about that, Maria.'

'Why else would he have done this? The castle was your wedding present.'

'He would never marry me.' Zoë tried to reason it out. She wanted nothing more than to accept that what Maria had said was true, made sense—but her mind just wouldn't accept it. Deep down she still believed she wasn't good enough. 'I could never—' She stopped, remembering Maria's history.

'Be his mistress?' Maria finished for her. 'As I was to his father? No, don't look so embarrassed, Zoë. You haven't offended me. I made my choice, and now you must make yours. But I can assure you Rico isn't looking for a mistress. He saw how unhappy it made his father. Yes.' She put her hand up when Zoë started to interrupt. 'Rico's father always wanted to marry me. He insisted my fears about our differing backgrounds were unfounded. He was ahead of his time; I was not. I know Rico loves you, Zoë. He wants you with him. He must have known how you would feel about such a life-change. He wanted you to keep your independence, your company—even your own accommodation, if that was what would make you happy.'

'A castle?' Zoë said wryly.

Maria sighed. 'Rico never does things by halves—and, after what you have told me today about your past, I think he wanted to protect you from uncertainty, do everything he could to reassure you. I think he loves you very much.' Maria's soft brown eyes bathed Zoë's face in compassion. 'And now you think it is too late. That is why you have come to me. You think you need my help.'

As their gazes locked, Zoë realised she had never needed anyone's help as much as she needed Maria's. 'I don't know what I can do to put things right,' she admitted huskily, 'or if it's possible to put things right.'

'You are strong enough to know what is right. You just

can't see it yet. You don't need me or your television company to cling to. You're a survivor, like me, Zoë. You know what you have to do.'

Zoë found Rico walking barefoot at the water's edge in front of the beach house. His jeans were rolled up and a soft breeze was lifting his blue-black hair as he faced the wind with his hands shoved deep inside his pockets.

She didn't have to see his face to know how much he was hurting—how much she had hurt him. There could be no more hiding inside the stockade. No more hiding, full stop. Reaching out, putting her heart on the same line as his, was exactly what she wanted to do.

'Zoë?' Rico whirled round with surprise. 'I thought you would have left for the airport by now.'

'Rico.' Zoë's heart lurched when she saw the weariness in his eyes. 'Can we talk?'

'Why not?' Opening his arms, he gestured around. 'There are only seabirds to hear us.'

Digging into the back pocket of her jeans, she pulled out the envelope. 'You didn't expect me to walk away after you left this at the castle?'

He didn't answer. He just folded his arms and stared at her.

'I've come to give it back to you.'

'That's a pity.' He looked at the envelope and turned it over in his hands. 'I grew up believing it was my destiny to own Castillo Cazulas. But when I brought it back into the family again I discovered it was just a large, empty building.'

'That's exactly what I thought when I locked it up just now.'

'When you were there the whole place was transformed.' Holding her gaze, Rico shook his head and smiled a smile that didn't quite make it to his eyes. 'Your programme, your team—you brought it back to life, Zoë. It was exactly what the old place needed.'

'Chaos?'

This time they both smiled.

Straightening the envelope he had tightly clenched in his fist, Rico held it out. 'When Castillo Cazulas was first built a whole community thrived there, not just one family. I want the castle to live again through you. Take it, Zoë. Castillo Cazulas is nothing without you. I'll probably sell it.'

'You can't give me a castle,' Zoë said incredulously. 'Rico, that's ridiculous.'

'That's what I keep telling myself.' He shrugged as he thrust the envelope into her hands.

Zoë shook her head. The only sound was the wind, and the sea pounding on the shore at their feet. 'I couldn't be in Cazulas, knowing I might see you, bump into you.'

'I don't want Castillo Cazulas for the very same reason,' Rico admitted. 'I could never see the castle now without thinking of you.'

'I'm sorry—this was a mistake. I should never have come.'

Turning, Zoë began walking quickly back across the sand towards the road, where she had left the car.

'Zoë—'

Rico's voice wavered on the wind, and then sank beneath the noise of the surf. Was this what she really wanted? Zoë wondered, her steps faltering. A lifetime of wondering, *What if?* A lifetime of running away from the past? A life without Rico in it? Hadn't the time come to stop running—to face up to life—to face him?

They both turned at the same moment.

Zoë didn't know who took the first step. She only knew that she was running with the wind at her back, and then Rico tasted of salt and sunshine, and when his arms closed around her she knew it was the only reassurance she would ever need.

The lease for Castillo Cazulas lay forgotten on the sand, and then the breeze picked it up and carried it away out to sea.

'You can't leave Cazulas, Zoë,' Rico said, pulling away

from her at last. 'We need you here. I need you. The village needs you. You're good for all of us. We love you. I love you. Please tell me you'll stay.'

'How can you ask me that when I've been so selfish—when I've hurt you so badly?'

'You haven't been selfish,' Rico assured her. Bringing her hands to his lips, he kissed them passionately. 'You were knocked down to the ground, Zoë. It takes time to grow straight again, to grow tall. But I'll wait for you for ever, if that's what it takes.'

Zoë was touched, dazed—even shamed by Rico's declaration. He saw so much where she had been blind. But her eyes were wide open now. This proud, passionate man was every bit as vulnerable when it came to love as she was.

Reaching up, she traced his cheek with her hand. 'I love you with all my heart, Rico. You've shown me what love should be, and I'll never leave you.' And she never would, Zoë realised; with or without his ring.

'I'm not asking you to give up anything, as long as you promise to leave some space in your life for me.'

'You've got it,' Zoë assured him. 'But it's a rather big space, if that's all right with you?'

'That's just perfect.' He dragged her close. 'Now, who shall we have to cater for the wedding?'

'The wedding?' Zoë stared incredulously into Rico's face as he heaved a mock sigh.

'I suppose you should have the night off on your wedding day.'

'Rico, what are you saying?'

'I'm saying the caterers will have quite a lot to live up to—'

'Rico!'

'Did I forget something?'

'You know you did!'

'Will you marry me, Zoë?' he said, growing suddenly serious. And when she just stared at him he knelt down in the wet sand and reached for her hand.

'You'll ruin your jeans—'

'Then say yes quickly, or I'll have to take them off.'

'Then it will take me a very long time indeed to accept your proposal.' Kneeling in front of him, Zoë put her hands in his. 'Yes, I'll marry you, Rico. And I'll love and honour and cherish you for ever—'

'There's just one condition for the wedding,' he cut in, drawing her close.

'Oh?' Zoë murmured against his mouth. 'What's that?'

'No cameras, *mi amor.*'

EPILOGUE

CAZULAS had never seen a wedding like it, the village *tio* assured Zoë excitedly. And they both agreed that it must be true when the King of Spain and his beautiful Queen attended the marriage ceremony—along with all of Zoë's friends and what seemed like half of Spain.

The dapple-grey horses that drew her wedding carriage had bells and ribbons bound through their glossy manes, and everything she wore for the wedding had been bought in Paris, where she had enjoyed a 'pre-marriage honeymoon', as Rico had insisted on referring to their trip.

Events had moved swiftly after that late afternoon together on the beach. It was the way they had both wanted it.

Breakfast in Madrid, lunch in Paris: Zoë discovered such things were commonplace in the life of El Señor Alarico Cortes de Aragon and his wife-to-be. To put the seal on their new life together, Rico never mentioned the little notebook Zoë took everywhere with her to jot down ideas for her new television series.

'Everyone in Cazulas can see that El Señor Alarico Cortes of Aragon has met his match,' the *tio* exclaimed, reclaiming Zoë's attention. 'Rico is very much in love.' He tapped the side of his nose in the familiar gesture.

'And I get to take the photographs,' Maria exclaimed, snapping away furiously.

'Are you really happy, Zoë?' Rico asked her later, when they danced together.

'Yes, I'm utterly, completely and totally happy. And as for this—' She gazed around at the glittering throng of friends and family Rico had assembled to celebrate their wedding day. 'This is *duende* for me—how about you?'

Rico drew her a little closer. 'Every moment I'm with you, Zoë, is a whole lot better than that.'

If you enjoyed what you just read,
then we've got an offer you can't resist!

Take 2 bestselling
love stories FREE!

Plus get a FREE surprise gift!

Welcome to a world filled with passion, romance and royals!

The Scorsolini Princes: Proud rulers and passionate lovers who need convenient wives!

HIS ROYAL LOVE-CHILD
by Lucy Monroe
June 2006

Danette Michaels knew that there
would be no marriage or future as Principe Marcello
Scorsolini's secret mistress. When she wanted more, the affair
ended. Until a pregnancy test changed everything...

Other titles from this new trilogy by Lucy Monroe
THE PRINCE'S VIRGIN WIFE—May
THE SCORSOLINI MARRIAGE BARGAIN—July

HPRB0606

Coming Next Month

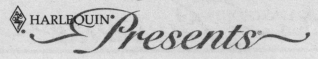
HARLEQUIN *Presents*

THE BEST HAS JUST GOTTEN BETTER!

#2541 HIS ROYAL LOVE-CHILD Lucy Monroe
Royal Brides

Danette Michaels knew that there would be no marriage, future or public acknowledgment as Principe Marcello Scorsolini's secret mistress. When she wanted more, the affair ended. Until a pregnancy test changed everything.

#2542 THE SHEIKH'S DISOBEDIENT BRIDE Jane Porter
Surrender to the Sheikh

He's a warrior who lives by the rules of the desert. When Sheikh Tair finds Tally has broken one of those sacred laws, he must act. Tally is kept like a slave girl, and her instinct is to flee, but as ruler, Tair must tame her. He knows he wants her—willing or not!

#2543 THE ITALIAN'S BLACKMAILED MISTRESS Jacqueline Baird
Bedded by Blackmail

For Max Quintano, blackmailing Sophie into becoming his mistress was simple: she'd do anything to protect her family from ruin—even give up her freedom to live in Max's Venetian palazzo. Now she's beholden to him, until she discovers exactly *why* he hates her so much.

#2544 WIFE AGAINST HER WILL Sara Craven
Wedlocked!

Darcy Langton is horrified when she finds herself engaged to arrogant, but sexy, businessman Joel Castille! But when Darcy makes a shocking discovery about her new husband, it's up to Joel to woo her back or risk losing his most valuable asset.

#2545 FOR REVENGE...OR PLEASURE? Trish Morey
For Love or Money

Jade Ferraro is a cosmetic surgeon, and Loukas Demakis is certain she's preying on the rich and famous of Beverly Hills to attract celebrity clients. He has no qualms about seducing information from Jade to uncover the truth.

#2546 HIS SECRETARY MISTRESS Chantelle Shaw
Mistress to a Millionaire

Jenna Deane is thrilled with her new job. Life hasn't been easy since her husband deserted her and their little daughter. But her new handsome boss expects Jenna to be available whenever he needs her. How can she tell him that she's a single mother?

HPCNM0506